THE F.A.R.T. FILES

Dr Rob Bell

He'll wrangle a snake, blow up a perfectly good can of chips, or even get flung around a theme park, all in the name of discovery. Dr Rob Bell is best known for donning his trusty white lab coat and jumping into science (sometimes literally), as the host of the kid's science TV show *Scope*. His enthusiasm for science is infectious, his curiosity is never-ending, but best of all he can relate it all in way that kids (and adults) understand and enjoy. He says that his love of science (and particularly the environment) came from growing up on a pineapple farm, where he became passionate about the impact that humans have on the environment and natural resources. It also gave him the chance to tinker with machines and just generally find out how stuff worked. Dr Rob has a Bachelor of Science with Honours and a PhD in materials chemistry from the University of Queensland. And it was at university that he also held another prestigious title, that of "President - The Chocolate Appreciation Society". He has worked as a Science Education Officer for the CSIRO, teaching students about science in the lab and at schools, and spent nearly eleven years hosting the (award-winning) *Scope*. He has been lucky enough to meet Nobel laureates, astronauts and sporting legends. He has seen a space shuttle up close and flown with a jetpack, but his favourite place is a grand ballroom carved completely out of rock salt in an underground mine in Poland. These days when he is not writing his first series of kids books, *The F.A.R.T. Files,* he is working on a science education website.

www.doctorrob.com.au

THE F.A.R.T. FILES 1

Dr Rob Bell

X

Disclaimer: All experiments and cooking featured in this book should be done under strict adult supervision. The publisher and author cannot be held responsible for any mess made!

First published under Xoum in 2018 by Brio Books

ISBN 9781925589351 (print)

Published in Australia and New Zealand by:

Brio Books, an imprint of Booktopia Group Ltd
Unit E1, 3-29 Birnie Avenue
Lidcombe, NSW 2141, Australia
Printed and bound in Australia by SOS Print + Media Group

The paper in this book is FSC® certified. FSC® promotes environmentally responsible, socially beneficial and economically viable management of the world's forests.

booktopia.com.au

This is for my favourite little elements Co, Se and Zr and my first critic Dave, who helped me avoid a black hole.

To the laws of physics, I would also like to say thanks, just for just being there (even if they do bring me down from time to time).

CONTENTS

Sommerton High

CHAPTER 1

Mysterious Messages

A lone figure lurked by the bag rack outside the classroom.

Shrouded in mystery.

Cloaked in secrecy.

The rest of Sommerton High was in class – as they should have been – so why was someone snooping around? They could, and probably would, get a detention if they were caught. But this nervous lurker was clearly on some kind of mission, scanning the school-bags quickly, looking for just the right one.

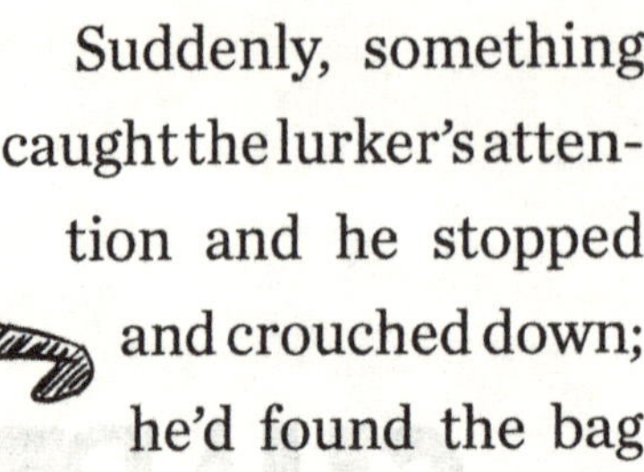

Suddenly, something caught the lurker's attention and he stopped and crouched down; he'd found the bag he'd been looking for. A glance at the name-tag confirmed the search was over. It simply read <Maddie>.

Ten minutes later, the scene was repeated outside another classroom. This time the bag belonged to Arlia Humphries. Had anyone witnessed this, they may have been surprised.

Why? Because nobody really knew Arlia.

Actually, that's not quite true. Arlia's parents knew her, of course, and so did the kids at her old school. But no one at Sommerton High *really* knew her – or so she thought.

When the bell rang for lunch, Arlia found her bag and was in the process of shoving books in and taking food out when she made a discovery.

Well, two discoveries, really.

The first discovery was that her rice cakes were crushed. She wasn't sure if it was her fault for packing too many books, or if it was the way she'd crammed her bag into the rack. Whatever the reason, her rice cakes now resembled breakfast cereal, without the milk. This was a major disappointment, because she loved her rice cakes. True, it was a craving nobody else seemed to understand, but it was a cheap and healthy addiction, so her parents were happy to keep her well supplied.

The crushed snacks were one discovery, and a rather sad one at that, but the second discovery was more puzzling. As Arlia pulled out the crumbly remains of her rice cakes, she noticed a fold-

Arlia

ed piece of paper. She hadn't put it there; she would have remembered if she had. Plus, it had her name on the outside, and who writes their own name on notes except people trying to seem popular on Valentine's Day?

No, this was no self-addressed love letter. So what was it?

Arlia read the note, or at least looked at it because you couldn't exactly *read* it. With a puzzled look on her face, she studied the piece of paper, turning it sideways and even flipping

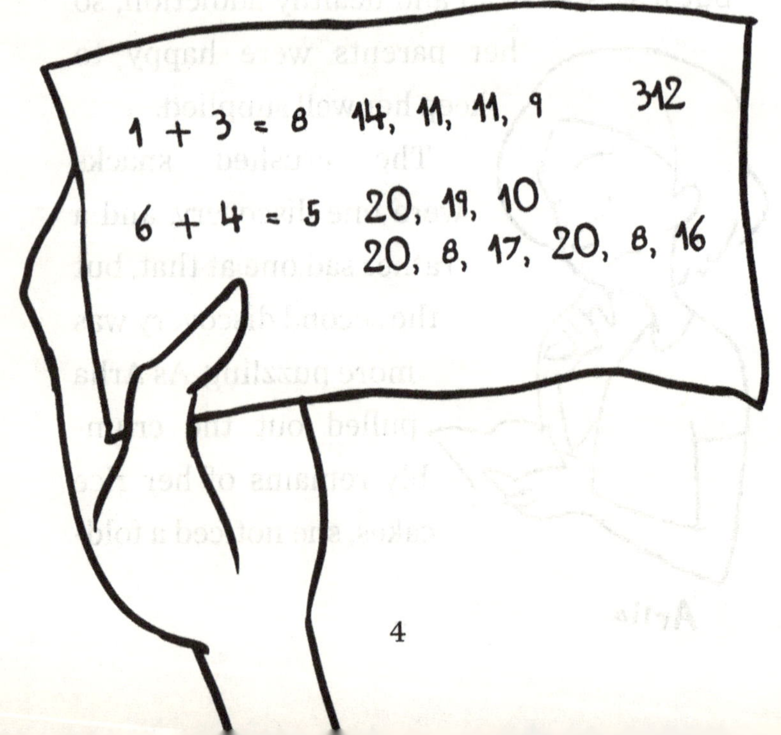

it over, as her mind went from baffled to curious. She decided, rightly or wrongly, that it was some kind of coded message, and she was determined to work it out.

On the other side of the school, Madison Litchfield was also going through her bag. Not that anyone called her Madison. Not even her parents when she was in trouble (which happened a lot). *Maddie* had grown up with a strong dislike of her full name, but was quite happy with the shortened version she had on her name-tag. Actually, she had two name-tags on her bag – <Maddie> and <@Maddie> – but that's not so important right now. What *is* important is that while looking for the USB stick that had her history assignment saved on it, she found *another* USB stick, one she didn't recognise. To some people, one USB stick may look like exactly like the next, but not to Maddie. She had a very good memory for these things. It was as if they were pets and she knew each one individually. So where had this light blue one come from? She held it up and asked if anybody owned it, but most of her classmates just looked at her blankly and then wandered off to eat.

Maddie looked at the USB again and noticed the letters "ML" on the side. Her initials. Weird. She put it in her pocket and continued looking for the USB with her assignment, although she couldn't help wondering where this extra drive had come from. In the dark depths of her bag she found a bit of dried-out orange skin, four hair elastics that had seen better days, two stubby pencils that had become too short to sharpen, and a fancy eraser that had once smelt like pineapples. Now it just smelt

of schoolbag. It went straight into the bin with all the other stuff.

Suddenly she remembered. The side pocket of her bag. She'd put the assignment USB there so it wouldn't get mixed up with the others. She retrieved it with a sigh of relief. Now she could relax and eat. Except there was still another mystery to solve ...

The light blue USB with "ML" on it.

She grabbed her sandwich and her computer tablet and decided to hang out somewhere quiet so she could get to the bottom of it all.

Meanwhile, Arlia had sat herself down, also somewhere quiet, and was madly scribbling

away with a pencil on some scrap paper. She had decided that the numbers on the mystery note were definitely *not* a maths problem and were therefore some kind of code. But how was she meant to crack it? She was mostly puzzled by the sums at the start of each line. For starters, they were wrong.

Her first thought was to try the obvious. Numbers representing letters. She quickly jotted out the alphabet, assigning each letter a number in order.

1 = A, 2 = B, and so on.

She went back to the note and tried to use her key to solve it. There was no letter for the number "312" so she treated the numbers "3", "1" and "2" individually. This gave "NKKI CAB" for the first line.

NKKI CAB

TSJ THQTHP

"Well, that seems like nonsense," she thought. She decided to do the second line to be sure. It came out as "TSJ THQTHP". Yep, nonsense. She stared at the note for a while, focusing her attention on the maths problems at the start of each line. They were clearly wrong, your average seven year old would know that, so why were they there? Then an idea hit her. What if the maths was somehow a clue to unlocking the code for that line? By combining her two ideas, she soon had the answer ...[1]

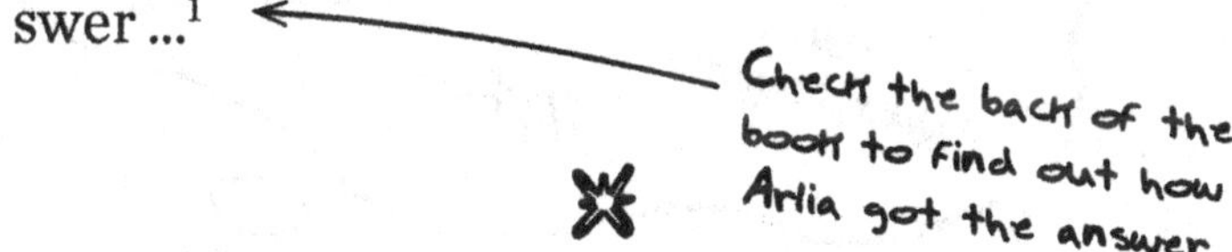

"Room CAF, one o'clock," she said quietly. She felt like she'd cracked the code now. Except for the CAF bit. Did it mean cafeteria? But the school didn't have a cafeteria, just a canteen. Then it dawned on her. The numbers 312 on the original note didn't stand for letters, they were meant to stay as numbers – it was supposed to be just 312. Room 312 was in the science block. And it seemed as if something was happening there at one o'clock. But what? Arlia had decoded one mystery, only to be presented with another.

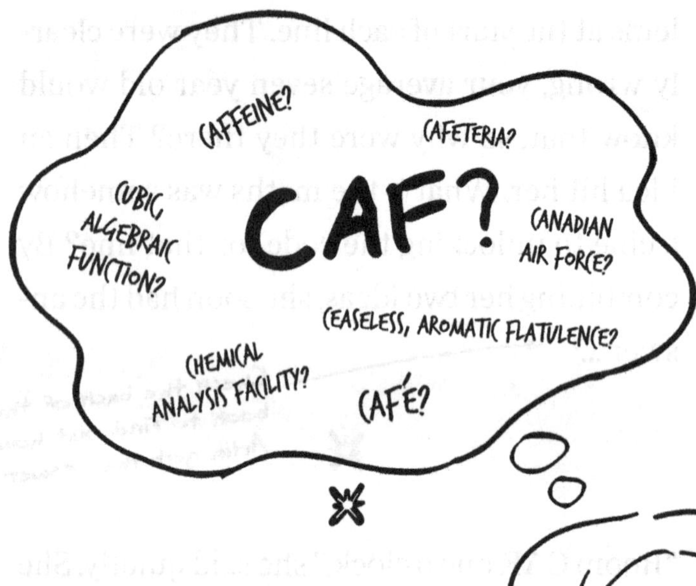

✲

Elsewhere, in a dark corner underneath the homeroom building, Maddie was wrestling with her own problem. She sat with her back against a wall and her tablet on her lap. She stared at the light-blue USB in her hand, almost as if she was trying to see through it.

"I don't remember you," she said to the portable memory stick. "Where did you come from?"

Maddie had a tendency to talk to herself, especially when she was trying to solve a mystery.

"Most likely, you belong to a fellow student with the same initials," she went on.

With a quick glance to confirm she was alone, Maddie logged into the school admin system and did a search of the student database for kids with the initials "ML". The search came back empty and Maddie logged out before she was discovered nosing around on the "staff only" site.

She twirled the USB stick around in her hand. There was only one thing

left to do: insert the stick into her tablet and see what was on it.

"But what if this is a trick?" she wondered. She stared at the USB again. "How do I know you're not carrying any viruses?"

After a few moments she shrugged and plugged the device in anyway.

"Oh," Maddie said, disappointed.

The drive was full of boring, pointless files. Machine-created code files for the most part. Thousands of them. No programs, no videos or pictures, just a lot of meaningless guff. She scrolled through the pages of file listings, scanning for anything unusual.

Then she saw it.

To most of us, it would have been like spotting a zebra with a few stripes more than the rest of the dazzle*. But to Maddie, it was like seeing a giraffe trying to blend in with bunch of zebras.

"Ah, what are *you* doing here?"

She opened it, and in the first line of code she saw this:

```
<Room 312, 1 pm>
```

Maddie tapped her lips in thought. It was 12.55 pm, but she was in no hurry. She unplugged the USB drive, tossed it in the nearest bin and picked up her lunch.

*A group of zebras is called a dazzle.

A **zebra** is basically a black-and-white striped horse. **But why do they have stripes?**

For many years, scientists believed it was to help them camouflage, or blend into their surroundings. In other words, so they could avoid being eaten by lions and hyenas. But that theory doesn't work so well when the animals move, which zebras do quite a bit. They become fairly visible. Also, when scientists studied how lions and hyenas see, it turns out they would smell the zebras before they saw them, so the stripes wouldn't make much difference hiding from a predator.

So **why??** There are still a few good theories. For starters, when a whole herd of zebras starts to run, it looks very confusing to other animals. Lines going everywhere! This is something known as dazzle camouflage. Another theory is that the zebra's stripes protect it against disease: insects that carry diseases struggle to land on their stripy skin and bite it.

If Maddie was feeling cool and calm, the boy running past the handball courts nearby was feeling anything but. He was round-faced, covered in freckles and had a bag half slung over his shoulder. His "run" was more a chaotic jog, as he attempted not to lose stuff from his bulging bag and pockets. The students who watched him dash past merely looked at each other and shrugged. Barely any of them knew who he was, let alone *why* he was running. But he did appear to be from their school, and he was headed for the science block.

In Room 312, one of the labs in the science block, the clock was about to strike 1 pm. The only people in the room – a student and a teacher – were both up the front, deep in conversation. The teacher was a tall, rather unusual-looking gentleman. He had a full head of messy white hair which was tinged with blue. His name was Mr Cobalt, and while

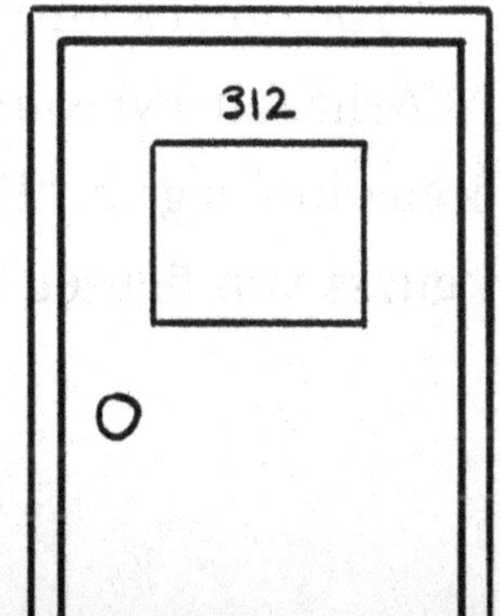

most students didn't know much about him, they all assumed his hair colour was the result of some chemistry experiment gone wrong.

Arlia knocked on the door. "Excuse me," she began.

Mr Cobalt turned towards her with a look so intense it froze Arlia to the spot. The boy merely smiled in her direction and nodded. Mr Cobalt muttered something to the boy, then straightened up, cleared his throat and said, "I'd better be going, nice to meet you." Arlia watched him walk down the corridor, feeling a bit stunned. She took a few steps into the room, still unsure if she was even meant to be there.

"Umm ... hi, I'm Arlia," she said hesitantly.

"You don't sound so sure," said the boy.

Arlia felt awkward, then saw the boy's face break into a grin. "I'm Sam," he went on. "So I guess you figured it out? Come and grab a seat. I'm expecting ... well, *hoping* for two more people to join us."

There were so many questions Arlia wanted to ask Sam, but she figured they would be answered soon enough, so she sat down. Sam looked familiar to her ... All of a sudden she realised it was Sam Tran from the year above. She didn't know that many people at Sommerton High, but Sam had won a dissection competition and his picture was up in the hallway near the biology room. It was hard to forget a smiling face posing right next to a toad with its insides displayed on the outside.

As Maddie climbed the stairs to the rooms on level 3, she was almost knocked over by the same boy she'd seen rushing through the school only minutes earlier. He was still all over the place, like a whirlwind, and his bag nearly caught Maddie as he flew by.

"Whoa, look out!" she said gruffly.

"Sorry," he called without turning around. "I'm late and a bit lost."

Maddie wasn't lost, but she was still wasn't sure if she wanted to do this. She peered through the little window in the door of Room 312. A girl she didn't know sat in a seat near the front, while a boy she *did* know sat on a desk nearby.

Just as she was about to enter, Maddie saw Mr Cobalt come out of a door a little further up the hallway. He stared at her briefly, raised his eyebrows in disbelief and then turned and walked in the opposite direction.

"Well, that wasn't weird," said Maddie sarcastically.

She sighed. She had come this far, she may as well go in and find out what was going on, even if it was some kind of prank.

“Hey, Maddie,” said Sam as she opened the door. “Glad you came along.”

“Yeah, well, you know, I had nothing else to do.”

Maddie sat down. She was about to reach for her tablet when the human whirlwind who had almost knocked her over burst through the door, puffing and panting.

“Sorry I’m late, I got lost!” he declared before slinging his bag to the floor and collapsing into a seat.

CHAPTER 2

It is *not* a club!

"That's everyone," said Sam, standing up and closing the door. "Firstly, Mr Cobalt has been pretty cool in letting us use this room, and he asked us not to mess with anything. Secondly, if you hadn't already figured it out, I was the one who scattered the breadcrumbs to lead you here today."

"Umm ... sorry to interrupt," said the human whirlwind, "but I didn't see any bread-crumbs on the way here. I mean, if there had been breadcrumbs, or even GPS coordinates,

I may not have run around so long trying to find this room."

"You know the school has maps all over it, right?" said Maddie.

"Maps? Who uses maps anymore?" The boy looked genuinely perplexed.

Arlia hid her smile.

"Okay," said Sam, a little confused. "Let me start over. When I said 'breadcrumbs', I meant *clues,* not actual crumbs of bread. I think the saying about breadcrumbs comes from *Hansel and Gretel.* They left breadcrumbs to help them find their way home. Just so we're clear, I didn't do that. For starters, there are too many pigeons around here. Also, I just wanted you three to turn up, not the whole school. That's why Arlia got the coded note, Maddie found an extra USB stick and you, Declan, were sent a book in the post."

The human whirlwind, aka Declan, thought for a moment. "Right ... okay, got it. Clues, not breadcrumbs. But I have one more question. Is this the room for detention? That's the reason I'm here. I have lunchtime detention today."

"No," replied Sam, looking confused again. "This is not the detention room."

"It used to be," clarified Maddie, "but they changed it this term to Room 306."

"There you go," said Sam. "Detention is in Room 306. This is Room 312. But you *are* Declan, right? I sent you a book of chemistry experiments?"

Declan began riffling through his bag. "A package in the post? Ah, now I checked our mailbox today as I left home, but it had been a while, lots of letters stuffed in there ... Wait, was it a small parcel for me? Maybe this is it?" He held up a brown package and then looked inside. "Yep, chemistry experiments. Nice, thanks. Wait ... why did you send me this?"

Sam looked like his head might explode. "You know what?" he said through tight lips. "It doesn't matter, just enjoy the book. And I guess you better get to Room 306 otherwise you'll end up with a double detention."

"No way!" cried Declan. "This seems way more interesting than detention. Secret stuff by invitation only, eh?"

"The idea was that only the people who solved their mysteries would actually turn up," said Sam. "That way they would have proved they're up to the task, which I will get to in a moment. But Declan, even though you were invited, you seem to be here by sheer accident."

"Yes, that is true," said Declan. "But if you give me a moment to figure it out, maybe I am up to the task of all this secret stuff, after all."

Sam didn't know what to say, but Declan wasn't waiting for an answer; he was already scouring through the experiment book. On page 13, he paused.

"Aha! There's a mistake here, made on purpose no doubt." He tapped the side of his nose. The others stared as once again he transformed into whirlwind mode, talking and moving about the room at great speed.

"On page 13 is the so called 'Elephant's Toothpaste' reaction, a classic demonstration of the power of a catalyst and exothermic decomposition. It says here to use 150 millilitres of hydrogen peroxide. That in itself is not strange ... Hmm, allow me to demonstrate, there must be some of this stuff around ...”

Before anyone could stop him, he had put on a lab coat and safety glasses and was doing the experiment.

“Okay, I’ve found some 30 per cent peroxide and I’ve set up two flasks, with some peroxide in each. Now the book says to add three drops of food colouring, one teaspoon of yeast, that’s the catalyst, but I’m using some KI, that’s potassium iodide I found instead, which is much easier. Lastly, it says add two drops of detergent.” He paused, hoping they could see what was obvious to him.

“You see, three drops, one teaspoon and two drops. *312*. The room number. And, of course, the whole thing is on page 13 ... 1300 hours is the same as 1 pm. But how did I know there was a mistake in this experiment?” The others stared at him blankly. "Because if you add them in the order it says here," he went on, "you get no foam, because the catalyst should go in last. Watch."

He added the chemicals to the two flasks. In the first flask he added them in the "wrong" order, and to the second he added them the "correct" way. The first flask puffed out some steam and the reaction caused a colourful splatter, as well as a yellowy brown stain and a bit of foam. Not exactly a dud, but not as good as the second flask. It immediately shot up a stream of brown-yellow foam with streaks of colour in it that reached a metre or two into the air before falling back onto the bench and floor. When it finished there was silence, and quite a lot of mess on the ceiling, floor and tables.[2]

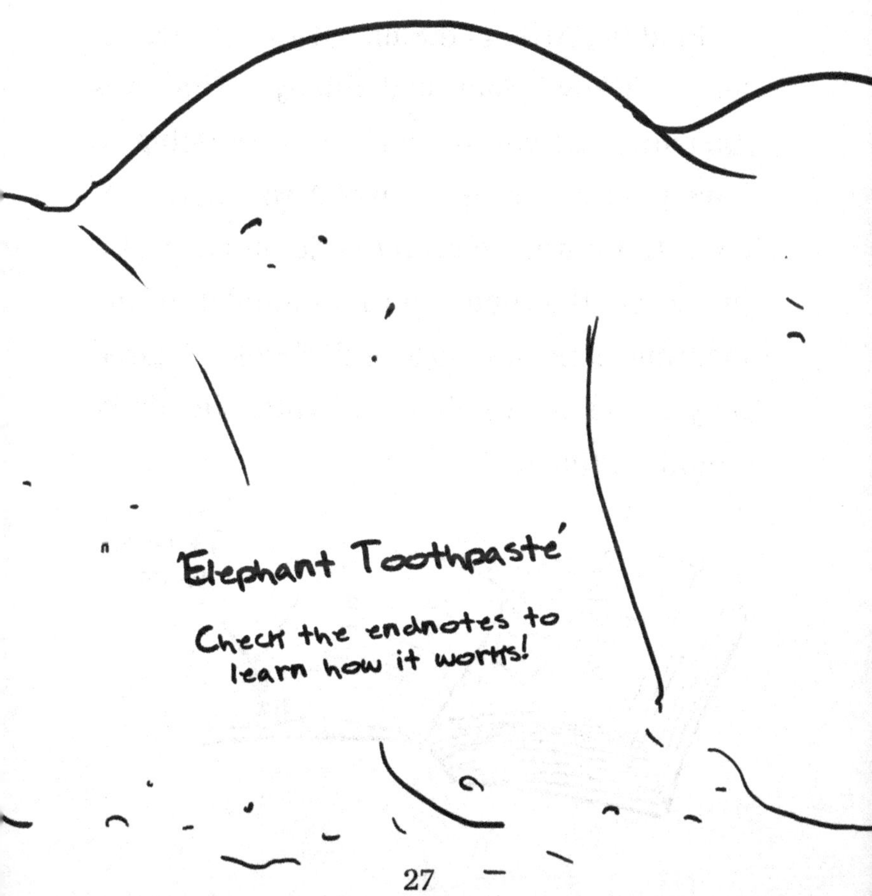

“Hmm, probably should have dialled back the amount of peroxide, but you get the idea, right?” Declan wiped the foam from his safety glasses so he could see.

Maddie, Arlia and Sam sat in stunned silence. “Okay,” Sam said finally. “That was amazing, but you do realise we’re going to have to clean up this mess? Also, for the record, there was no secret code on page 13. I just wrote the time and room number of the meeting on the last page of the book. I figured only someone who’s really into chemistry would get that far.”

"Oh right," said Declan as he flicked to the end of the book. "Yep, there it is, I see it now. Room 312, 1 pm ... Well, I feel like a bit of a goose!"

"Don't sweat it, that was great," said Sam. "It told me all I needed to know. Maybe you can start cleaning up while I start explaining everything else."

Sam began by saying that he had wanted to recruit some of the smartest kids in the school. He could have picked the people with the best marks, but he wanted people who could think *laterally*. Outside the box. Join the dots together. Follow the breadcrumbs (not real ones, of course). But why did he want to create this crack squad of problem solvers? He was just about to get to that when there was a knock at the door.

"If that's a teacher, I didn't make this mess,

okay? I found it like this and I'm cleaning it up," said Declan, dumping another load of coloured, foamy paper towel in the bin.

But it wasn't a teacher.

"Sam, there's a small version of you here with some paper bags," said Maddie by the door. "He says they contain food."

The kid was Dan Tran, Sam's younger brother, and he'd brought food from their mother. Mrs Tran was Vietnamese and believed that her boys needed home-cooked meals for lunch every day, even when they were at school.

Sam took the bags from Dan and waved his brother goodbye. He spread out food containers on the table.

"What is it?" asked Arlia, picking up a small fried pastry parcel.

"Smells like deep fried duck poo," said Declan from the sink on the other side of the room.

"Are you making fun of my mum's cooking?" asked Sam, mock serious.

"Ah, no, I just, was, you know ..." Declan turned red.

"It's fine, dude, really. If you don't like it, you don't have to eat it. I love it, so I'll have your share." Sam crunched into one of the snacks. "And yes, actually it *is* deep fried duck poo!"

Just as he said it, Maddie and Arlia had each taken a large bite. Arlia turned pale and Maddie spat her food into her hand. Sam began to laugh. "You really think my mum would send me that? They're just prawn and pork dumplings. You should have seen your faces."

Arlia forced a smiled and slowly continued chewing.

Maddie just rolled her eyes.

"Still, it's not that weird, is it? I mean, some animals do actually eat poo ..." Sam was about to say more, but he could tell by the looks on the girls' faces that he should stop. For a while the group ate in contented silence.

Did you know

that mother koalas, elephants and pandas feed their babies a special kind of poo when it is time to move from milk to solid food?

For their babies to be able to live on very specific diets (like bamboo for pandas), their guts have to contain the right mix of bacteria. The gut bacteria help with digestion and getting the maximum nutrition out of the food. But how do you get these crucial bacteria into a baby koala's gut, for example? Well, the mother koala feeds a special kind of koala number two called "pap" to the baby, and the rest is gum-leaf-munching history.

Scientists think that maybe it's not just these animals that could benefit from this kind of thing. We are just beginning to discover the importance human gut bacteria play in many parts of our lives, not just digesting food. Indeed, for certain kinds of sickness, one of the best treatments can be a poo transplant from a healthy person! Technically it is known as "Fecal Microbiota Transplant" or FMT. It can help to build up the population of helpful bacteria in the sick person's gut, and make them better. It goes in via a tube, though, so thankfully no eating is involved.

"I hate to get us back on topic, but what exactly are we here for?" asked Maddie finally. "No offence, but it seems like you're trying to start a science club, and I don't do clubs."

"No, no," Sam said. "It's nothing like that. I was hoping you guys could help me solve a problem that has the experts baffled."

This got everyone's attention. There was nothing more intriguing to a smart kid than the idea of solving something others couldn't. Especially if those others were experts!

CHAPTER 3

Now for a case to solve

Sam paused to let his statement sink in. Just as he was about to continue, Arlia leant over and picked up the local paper which was lying on the front desk. "You mean investigate something like this?" she said, pointing to a photo on the front page. It showed a group of sad-looking soccer players standing next to their clubhouse. It had been broken into and there was graffiti everywhere, plus someone had left deep tyre tracks on the oval. The headline read:

THE SOMMERTON DAILY
LOCAL CLUB GETS A KICKING
Loserz

Sam shook his head without looking at the article. "Before we get carried away solving the world's problems, I was hoping you guys could help me work out who broke into and vandalised a building at my soccer club."

Arlia looked confused, but Maddie grinned. She nudged Arlia, who quickly caught on. "I think we should go with *Arlia's* idea," Maddie said, her eyes sparkling. "What do you think, Declan?" She turned to him with a look that said, trust me, this will be funny.

"Sure," said Declan, as he realised what the girls were up to. "The story in the paper is both heart wrenching and local. It deserves our attention."

Sam was lost for words. "Okay, um, but you see I really just wanted to ..." Maddie jumped up and held the paper in front of his face, forcing him to look at it properly. "Oh, right ... very funny. That's the same thing I was talking about – that's my club."

"So, do you think we can be sort of like police, or forensic investigators?" asked Arlia.

"What about the real police?" asked Declan.

"They came and listened to the complaint and wrote a report, but that was it," said Sam.

"Yeah, they don't send the forensics team out to every little thing," Maddie said. "They just do the big stuff. Hmm ... Wait a minute, let me make a quick call."

She reached into her bag and grabbed her phone. At the same time, with her other hand, she was tapping away on her tablet. After a few moments, she called someone and waited for them to answer.

“Hello, this is Ingrid Bowman from the Brownleigh Football Club,” Maddie said, sounding much older. “I was hoping to speak to the detective in charge of our vandalism complaint; the insurance company would like to know when the report is coming.”

Everybody stared at Maddie with their mouths open, then looked at each other. Declan mouthed the words: “the police!”

Maddie ignored them and continued talking. "I see, thank you, and can I confirm that the investigation is no longer ongoing? Well, that is a shame but we understand. Goodbye." She ended the call, looked up at the others and, without missing a beat, said, "The police are done with it, like I thought. But I reckon if we can find some evidence, something we can prove, they'll listen to us. Wanna meet at the soccer clubhouse this afternoon?"

"Umm, sure," said Sam, a little stunned. He turned to Arlia and Declan and they both nodded their agreement.

"Bring whatever you think might help," Sam added.

Declan had been busy jotting down notes on a piece of paper. As they got up to leave, he said, "Now, I know we're not forming a *club*, as such, but I thought it might be nice for us to have a name. And I've come up with one ... Ready? Wait for it ... the Forensic Amateur Research Team!"

Maddie shrugged. "Whatever floats your boat. Actually, speaking of names, you're Declan Peterson, right?" She was studying her tablet again.

Declan nodded, looking wary. "Why?"

"I just think it's weird that you go to this school but I've never seen you before. I mean, I don't notice everyone, but where have you been? You're absent a lot, but still passing exams?"

Student record:

- truancy
- making a mess
- that's it

Declan Peterson

"I study a lot from home, it's easier," said Declan. "And the school have been understanding ... Oh, and while you're logged into the school admin, can you maybe carve a few days off my absentee list?"

Maddie blushed and quickly shut down her tablet.

"Right, well, thanks for turning up today, guys," said Sam. "I'll see you all this afternoon." He started clearing up the empty food containers.

As Maddie, Arlia and Declan headed out for what was left of lunchtime, they passed Mr Cobalt heading in the opposite direction.

"Do you guys know if the tuckshop is still open?" asked Declan. "And if so, where is it?"

Before either girl could answer, they heard a voice coming from Room 312.

"What in the seven seas happened here? And why is half the peroxide missing?"

Maddie peeked in the window. Mr Cobalt was talking to Sam. He didn't look happy, but he didn't look angry either, which was a bit odd considering his discovery.

"On second thoughts, I might just catch the end of detention," said Declan before he turned and hurried off down the corridor.

"Hey wait!" Arlia called after him. "It's not that way, it's this way. Also, I've got something for you." She handed Declan a piece of paper containing sets of numbers.

"If this is some kind of coded message, I give up now," said Declan. "Numbers aren't my thing, I'm better with chemicals ... well, most of the time."

"It's not a coded message, it's the GPS coordinates for the soccer club, in case the pigeons eat the breadcrumbs!"

CHAPTER 4

Hippos and whales?

Straight after school, Sam got on his bike and rode to the soccer club. Maddie and Arlia took the bus, and Declan just kind of appeared there, out of breath. He said it was because he had walked, but there did seem to be a person in a car waving to him as they drove away from the bottom of the hill.

“Maybe I’ve watched too much TV, but I figured if we find anything useful, we should copy what the professionals do and take some photos, then bag up the evidence,” Sam said,

producing some large snap-lock bags.

"You probably *have* been watching too much TV," said Maddie. "I mean, those forensic shows are pretty unrealistic. But it can't hurt to keep a record of anything we find." She realised Sam was just trying to help and didn't want to dampen his enthusiasm with reality. She had a habit of doing that to people. "I can set up a shared cloud directory; I'll ping you all the details. If you find something, make sure you take a photo with your phone and make sure it's geo-tagged, so we know exactly where you took it."

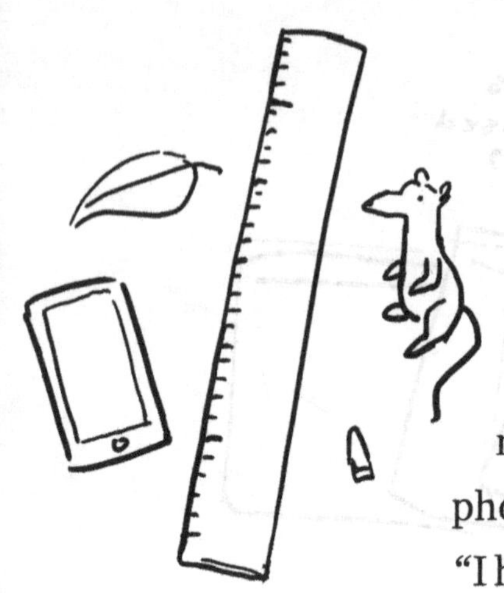

"Also," chimed in Arlia, "it might be a good idea to have some scale to the photos, so if you have a ruler, put that near the thing you are photographing."

"I have definitely seen them do that on TV and in crime movies," said Declan. "And ..." he looked excited, "they also wear those full body suits so their DNA doesn't contaminate the scene!"

Deoxyribonucleic acid, or DNA for short.

Everyone agreed the suits were a great idea, but perhaps a bit impractical, given the heat ... and the fact that no one knew where to get them ... and that they weren't really trying to find DNA, anyway.

Sam explained that the break-in and vandalism at the soccer club had occurred two nights ago, so it was quite likely that other people had been there since. Maybe the scene wasn't exactly as it had been left that night, but they could still have a good look. They split up to hunt for clues.

Maddie and Arlia went down to the field to take pictures of the tyre tracks and skid marks while Declan and Sam stayed at the clubhouse. Suddenly, there was an excited yelp from Declan, who'd gone around the back of the building and was searching among some bushes. Sam came to see what the fuss was about.

"I've found the footprint of a hippo!" Declan cried from somewhere deep within the shrubbery.

"Um, a few questions spring to mind, Declan," said Sam. "Is there more than one footprint? Because I'm fairly sure hippos have four legs, and can't hop on just one. Are there any toe prints? Hippos have four toes. Also, as far as I know, there aren't any hippos living outside of zoos in this country ..."

"Okay, so maybe it isn't a hippo footprint," said Declan, "but something round-ish has pressed into the ground here ... Oh, and Sam? You seem to know a lot about hippopotamuses."

"What can I say?" replied Sam. "They're cool animals. Their closest living relatives are dolphins and whales, they can sleep underwater, despite being air breathers, and they kind of sweat out this red stuff, which is their own self-applying sunscreen."

There's no doubt about it, hippos are odd creatures. By tracing their genetic family tree and looking at fossils, scientists think hippos and the cetaceans (whales and dolphins) had a common ancestor some 60 million years ago. Unlike whales and dolphins, hippos are only semi-aquatic. This means they spend *most* of their life in water, (the rivers of Africa, to be precise), but do come out sometimes, like at sundown, to eat grass. Amazingly, they go underwater to have a sleep, and they can automatically come up to breathe without waking up. Because they spend so much time in the water, their skin can dry out or get sunburnt easily. To help stop that happening, they ooze a fluid out of their skin that turns red, acts as a sunscreen and helps stops bad bacteria living in any cuts. People used to think it was blood from a hippo battle (these happen between males), but now the stuff is even being researched to make better human sunscreens.

Finally, when male hippos go to the toilet, it's not pretty. They spin their little tails like a helicopter to fling the poo all around the place, marking their territory.

Declan was impressed, but he was more interested in working out what might have made the mark in the dried-up mud. He spied an old paint tin in the bushes. It didn't look as if it had been used recently, but he lifted it up and immediately noticed it fitted the round mud mould perfectly. He thought for a moment, then looked up. Above him, in line

big paint bucket

with the paint tin, was a small window. He figured someone had been trying to reach the window, probably by standing on the tin. But the window was firmly shut, and judging by the spider webs it had been shut for a while. It looked like a dead end.

"Just a red herring as it turned out," he said, emerging from the bushes with the paint tin in his hand.

"First it was a hippo and now it's a herring? How can a fish make a footprint?" asked Sam, confused.

"I said 'red herring'," Declan explained. "It is an expression. It means it's a dead end, not a real clue, just something that might put us off track. I think someone stood on the tin to try to get in the window. But then they couldn't, so that's it."

Sam was only half-listening. "No, that's not it. There's

something fishy about your red herring. Look, there's mud on top of the tin and it looks to me like it's a smudgy part-footprint. Like someone was standing on the tin on their tiptoes. Put a ruler next to it, Declan; this deserves a photo!"

Meanwhile, down on the oval, Maddie and Arlia had just finished taking pictures of the tyre tracks. The tracks crisscrossed and went in circles, as though someone had hooned around, ripping up the grass and making a mess of the place. There weren't many places where the tyres had left clear tracks, but they managed to find a couple in softer ground that may have been mud a couple of days ago. As they walked back up to the clubhouse, they could see the boys excitedly photographing an old paint tin.

"What are they doing?" said Maddie.

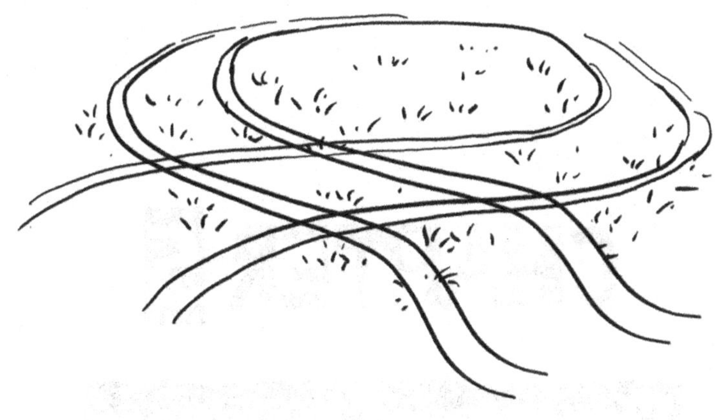

"Taking a picture of an old paint tin, I think," said Arlia, stating the obvious. "What are we going to do with all this?"

"Excellent question," said Maddie. "Tyre tracks are all the same to me, but I figure we have a good look around and try to find and record as much stuff as we can. Anything that might help. Then we'll just have to think, research a bit, think some more ... and hope we come up with something."

CHAPTER 5

Popcorn and asparagus

Back at the clubhouse, they compared their findings and uploaded them to the online space Maddie had set up earlier. It was fair to say everyone was a bit disappointed by what they had found so far, but they were determined to keep looking. Maddie suggested that she photograph all the graffiti (there was quite a bit of it) and Sam offered to help. Arlia was keen to study a roller door that had been prised open, because although it had since been fixed, the scars of the break-in remained.

Declan set off to check out the grassy area between the clubhouse and the creek – if nothing else, he figured the culprits might have dumped some empty spray cans down there.

After a good fifteen minutes of investigating, Maddie, Arlia and Sam headed down to join Declan as he traipsed through the grass and trees. When they reached him, he was sitting down and looking puzzled.

"What is it?" asked Sam.

Declan sighed. "Well, I can tell you what it was, and it *was* a fire. Not a very big one, a few small sticks and biggish bits of wood. I'd say it was pretty recent; it could have been the people who did all the damage. Just one thing puzzles me, though: the fire clearly stopped suddenly, *very* suddenly. This plastic thing was in the middle, where it would have been hot, but it has only melted a bit. It's like something put out the fire instantly."

Sam was first with a possible solution. "What about rain? It has definitely rained in the past few days, maybe the fire was only just going when it started?"

But then Maddie pointed out that the rain came before the vandals. That's why there were muddy footprints and soft ground for the tyre tracks. By now Arlia was studying the partly melted small red plastic object Declan had found in the ashes, but she couldn't identify it so passed it on to Maddie.

"This is, well, it *was*, the nozzle of a can of spray paint," Maddie declared.

Sam grinned. Another clue. "You're right, the red of the nozzle definitely matches one of the colours painted on the clubhouse. But where's the can?"

"I know what happened," answered Arlia.

"Well, I *think* I know what happened ... It's like popcorn."

"Huh?" said Declan.

"I think they tossed an almost empty spray can on the fire," Arlia explained. "As the gas inside heated up, it expanded and made the can into a tiny pressure bomb. First the lid popped off, like a safety valve, then the thing exploded. Kind of like popcorn. When you heat a corn kernel, the water inside turns to steam and it eventually builds up so much pressure it blows apart, making the corn pop.

But in this case, I think the can explosion blew out the fire too, just like a candle on a cake."

Putting out fires using explosions is actually a real thing. It's mostly used for fires at oil and gas wells, because they burn so ferociously and are very hard to extinguish otherwise. The shock wave from the controlled and well-directed explosion blasts the flames from the fuel source, and the in-rushing air stops it from re-lighting. There has even been research done to see if explosions can be used to help stop fierce bushfires. But for now, the closest we get to that is water bombing.

The other three looked at each other and nodded approvingly. It was a plausible explanation. It also meant that, unless the vandals had cleaned up after themselves, the exploded can was probably still around there somewhere.

They fanned out to quickly search the area, and it was Maddie who made the first discovery, although not the one she had hoped to make.

"Hey!" she shouted, scrunching up her nose. "Something smells fishy over here."

"Maybe it's another red herring!" shouted Declan, chuckling to himself. But as he turned and walked towards Maddie, his smile faded. His mind flashed back to two very recent events that had led to his current unfortunate predicament.

The first was that he'd had asparagus rolls for lunch. For those of you who don't know, these are usually made by taking

Declan's didn't have the fancy olive

spears of tinned asparagus, wrapping them in buttered white bread, and securing it all with a toothpick. Declan had become obsessed with them at a party his parents had taken him to, and now he made them at home from time to time.

The second thing was more recent; in fact, it happened just after he wandered down to the grassy area. He realised he hadn't been to the toilet all afternoon, and now he was busting. The sound of the nearby stream hadn't helped. So he'd snuck off behind a tree and done a very long, satisfying wee.

And yes, this was the same tree that Maddie was now standing next to.

"Maddie, um, don't go ... I mean, don't move. Just walk back this way," Declan stammered. Maddie stayed where she was and stared at him, bewildered. Declan tried again. "What I am trying to say is, I had asparagus for lunch ..."

Now Maddie and Arlia were both staring at him, utterly confused. Sam, on the other hand, had worked out what Declan was about to say. "Oh no," he said, smiling to himself.

"The thing is," Declan went on, "when I got down here, I really had to go ... you know, have a whiz, so I picked an out-of-the-way spot, and, well, it was there." He pointed at the tree as he spoke.

Maddie made a disgusted face and sprinted, with high knee lifts like she was running over a floor covered in honey, back to where the fire had been. Arlia turned around so Maddie wouldn't see her trying desperately not to laugh.

As Sam jogged over towards Maddie, he accidentally "kicked the can".

Now, sometimes adults might use this expression to say that someone is procrastinating, or avoiding doing their work. But in this case, it meant that Sam *actually* kicked the can (well, the exploded remains of a red spray paint can).

Sam showed the exploded can to the others. They all agreed they had a pretty good haul of clues, so they decided that was enough for one day. Besides, Arlia had a piano lesson, Declan had homework, Sam had to help his parents and Maddie just wanted to have a shower.

As they walked back to the clubhouse, Arlia asked Declan quietly, “Hey, why did you mention you had asparagus for lunch?”

Sam overheard and cleared things up. “Asparagus makes your wee smell really weird. A kind of sulphur-type smell. Except, some people don’t make the smell, and some people make it but can’t smell it. It’s pretty strange.”

Mercaptan
The chemical in asparagus pee that makes it (and farts) smell.

“I don’t think I’ve ever eaten asparagus before,”

said Arlia, "but I'm definitely going to get some and try it out."

Maddie had also heard the conversation and was frowning.

"Just so you know," she began, "that whole experience was pretty disgusting, so I'd rather you guys didn't talk about it. At least not while I'm still here."

As a peace offering, Declan suggested they all meet up at his place tomorrow. They could use the shed at the side of his house.

"It can be kind of like our clubhouse," he added, then remembered Maddie's views on clubs. "Or not ... you know, it doesn't matter, but I have a load of stuff in there, like wi-fi, air-conditioning, and my parents will leave us alone ..."

"Sure, whatever, email or text me the details," Maddie said as she walked off towards the bus stop, not even bothering to turn around.

The others waved Declan goodbye and were a good distance away before he finally found what he had been looking for in his bag.

"I guess now is not the time to show you the business cards I had made?" he said aloud, knowing no one would hear him. He looked down at the cards briefly, before smiling, stuffing them back in his bag and heading off home.

CHAPTER 6

Perps and pancakes

It was a truly beautiful Saturday morning. The sun was shining, the birds were singing, and all that other stuff that is supposed to make a day brilliant – well, it was probably happening too. But inside a shed attached to the side of a large, red-brick house, there were four people not yet interested in enjoying the day.

Actually, calling it a "shed" is misleading. Declan called it that, but his parents had decked it out with everything their only child might want – including a ping-pong table and a TV – so it was quite liveable. In fact, Declan often did live in his shed. His parents weren't around that much – they had busy jobs at the university – and he preferred it to the empty house.

Declan's ping-pong table was currently covered with the evidence the team had collected from the soccer club. Sam had even printed out a few of the more interesting photos they'd taken.

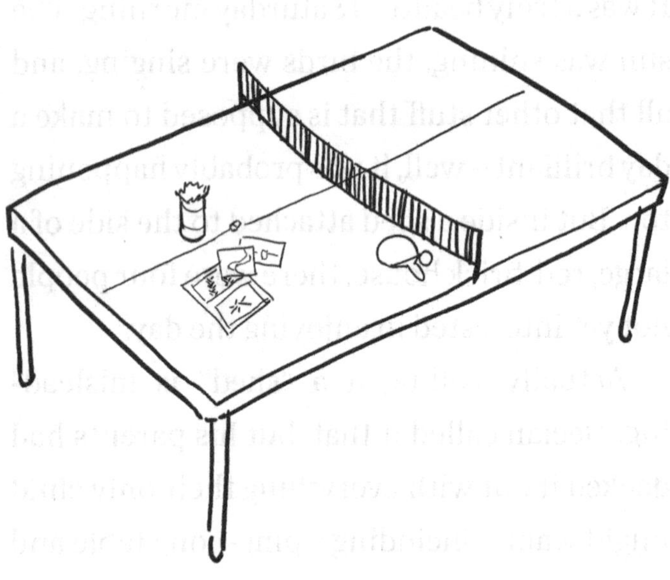

"Okay, so how do we start making some sense of all this? Any suggestions?" he asked.

When neither of the girls answered, Declan spoke up. "I spent last night doing some research," he told them. "I watched a few different crime shows where they use forensic science to try to solve a mystery. I also watched this strange Korean cartoon about magical talking cabbages. I'm still not sure exactly what was going on there ... But in all the cop shows, the first thing they do is get a whiteboard and start mapping it out."

With that, Declan jumped up and grabbed a sheet that was draped over something next to him. The idea was to reveal the whiteboard he'd positioned underneath, but he hadn't practised the move and the sheet caught on the top corners of the board. As a result, there was no dramatic reveal, but rather a giant crash, as the whiteboard and sheet tumbled to the ground. Declan tried to catch it as it fell, but ended up under it.

"Okay, that didn't happen in the TV shows!"

As Declan climbed out from under the whiteboard, Sam decided to float an idea.

"How about we go through each bit of evidence we found and work out how it might help us find the person – or people – who broke into the clubhouse."

"Perps," said Declan, struggling to stand the whiteboard back up.

"Sorry ... what?" asked Sam.

"*Perps,*" repeated Declan. "It's the slang they use on TV for the criminals. Weird word, huh? I had to look it up, but it turns out it's just short for *perpetrators*."

"Sure," said Maddie with an American accent, sounding like one of the characters on a cop show. "Let's nail these perps! Whatta ya got for me, chief?"

Once they had all had a go at pretending to be characters from a cop show, they decided that using the whiteboard was probably a good idea, after all. Sam began by drawing the outline of a person's head with a large question mark inside it.

"Okay, so this is our 'perp'," he said. "And down here I'm going to write all the things that may lead us to him or her."

He listed all the things they had got from the soccer club, spacing the words across the width of the board. "Lastly, we need to work out how we can connect any of these things to an actual person. What can the evidence tell us about the perp?"

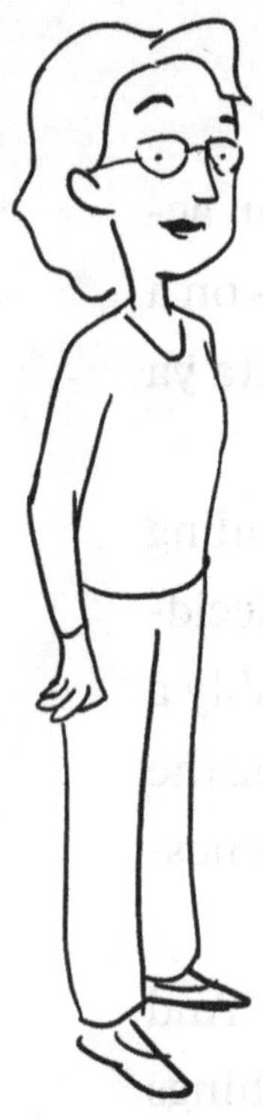

Arlia picked up one of the photos of the tyre tracks. "I think ..." she began when there was a knock on the shed door. Declan hopped up to see who it was.

"Oh, hi Mum," he said.

"Hello dear," she replied. "I know you said not to interrupt, but another of your little friends has arrived, so I thought I would show him through." She lowered her voice and tried to whisper, "Although to be honest, I thought I'd already met this boy this morning."

Declan turned to the others with a puzzled look on his face. It all made sense when Sam's younger brother, Dan Tran, stepped out from behind Declan's mum with a giant smile on his face.

"So this is your new secret club?" he said to Sam.

"What are you doing here?" Sam said. "How did you even know where I was?" Sam stopped and sniffed the air. "Is that pancakes I can smell?"

Dan looked smug. "I brought you some food – Mum's idea not mine. I knew where you were from a search you did on the computer before you left. And your bike is parked out front, so that made it easier. And yep, that's pancakes you can smell, there's some dipping sauce too."

Dan reached into his backpack and pulled out two bags of food, and began arranging it all on the ping-pong table. He'd even brought serviettes.

"Okay, you can leave the food, but you have to go," said Sam. "I'm going to text Mum and tell her you've left. She'll get worried if you don't turn up soon." Sam was happy to see the food, but he didn't want his little brother sticking around – even if he had shown himself to be quite a resourceful little detective in finding Declan's shed.

"Oh yeah, and it's not a club, either," said Declan as Dan was leaving. "I guess it's more like a team thing?" he said to himself.

Everyone's attention quickly turned to the pancakes. They were all hungry, but only Sam was eating. He realised a short explanation was necessary.

"They're kind of a savoury pancake. I think these ones have spring onion and squid in them. You can add green stuff from that container if you want, and I really like the dipping sauce."[3]

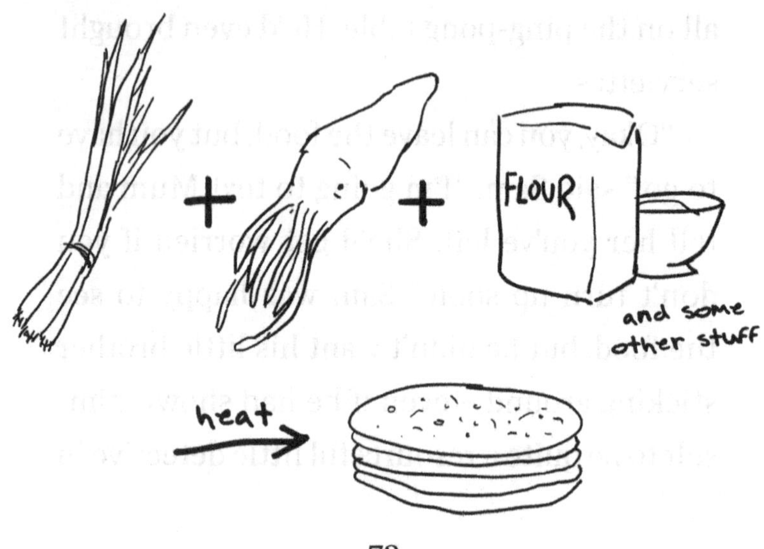

It didn't take long before everyone was scarfing down the pancakes and loving them. The chilli in the dipping sauce was turning Arlia bright red, but it didn't stop her from eating her fair share.

Once they were all full, their attention turned again to the whiteboard of clues and trying to solve the mystery.

"If someone was driving a car over the soccer fields," Declan said, "then they probably have a licence, right? And it's probably *their* car."

"Makes sense," said Sam. "But we have to be careful what we assume. The evidence only tells us that this person, or people I guess, had access to some kind of car."

"We do know a little about the car," said Arlia. "If you look at the photos, you can see the pattern of the tyre tread and measure the width of the tyre. Based on trawling through way too many tyre websites last night, I'd say they are a performance tyre, maybe a Pirelli. And they're a bit old, because the tyre tread that left the tracks was a bit worn. They're also 215 millimetres wide, which narrows down the kind of car they would be on."

"This is great," said Sam, writing down the main points on the whiteboard. "I never knew tyres could tell you so much!"

A 'tyresome' conversation

CHAPTER 7

Red is not just Red

"You know how we took photos of all that graffiti we saw?" asked Maddie. "Well, ever since then, I seem to notice graffiti all over the place."

"Especially around the train line," said Arlia.

"Yeah, right," said Maddie. "The thing is, I have noticed in some places really similar things to what we saw sprayed on the clubhouse. I took a few more pictures. My point is, I think this is not their first crack at graffiti."

"What if we could identify all the graffiti around town that matched the soccer club graffiti and map out where it was?" Declan asked. "That might give us an idea where the perp lives, or works, or even just where they get their paint?"

Maddie clicked her fingers and sat up straight. "Good idea. And, even better, we don't have to go out and physically look for it all. What about using image recognition software? I think I could make something that would automatically search and then find matches between the club graffiti and graffiti around town."

Everybody stared at her blankly. Was Maddie talking about sending out a robot to take photos of graffiti?

Maddie sighed. "It works like this," she explained. "I find a computer program that can be taught to identify imag-

es that are similar to a source image. Kind of like how your phone or even Facebook can find your face among random photos. In our case, I would feed it the graffiti patterns we have from the soccer club, and it can scan street view images from all around the neighbourhood looking for matches."

"Awesome idea, Maddie," said Sam. "How long will it take to write the program, though?"

"Oh, I'm not going to write it. That would be super complicated and take a long time, but there's plenty of stuff already out there. I just need to tweak it a bit. I'll put my feelers out tonight and should have some results pretty soon."

Feeling good about their progress so far, they moved on to the other clues. The photos of the roller door that had been levered open didn't tell them much. Declan pointed out that, judging by the marks left in the paint, it was most likely done using a flat-bladed screwdriver. The trouble was, those kinds of screwdrivers are very common, so it didn't seem to help.

There was a photo of a combination lock next. It was the lock on the equipment room, a room that wasn't even broken into. "I'm not sure who took the photo, but nothing was missing from the equipment room," said Sam. "I don't know what it can tell us."

"I took the photo," said Arlia, quietly. "I didn't know it was the equipment room; I just thought it was odd they hadn't tried to open it. So maybe they knew it was an equipment room, and not worth breaking into. Maybe one of them had played soccer there."

"Ooh, an *inside job*. I love it!" cried Declan.

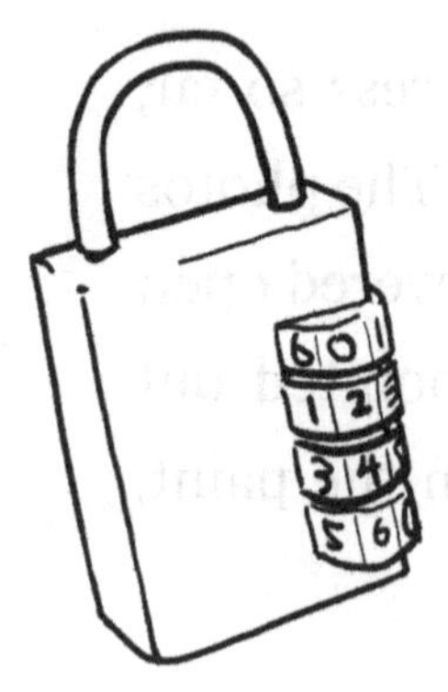

"Or maybe it just was going to take too long to crack a combo lock?" said Sam, playing devil's advocate. "I mean, do you know how many combinations there are?"

"Yes," said Arlia, even though Sam wasn't expecting an answer. "For that lock there are 2401 combinations. If you could check one combination every one to two seconds, which is realistic, it'd take you about an hour to get through them all. I'm sure no one is that patient, but when people lock these up they usually just give them a quick spin, so that cuts down the number of options. You have just two or three likely numbers on each wheel, so say 81 combinations. Plus the little wheels wriggle a bit when you are on the right number."

"Right ..." said Sam, not sure how to respond. Arlia sure knew her numbers. "You don't think they even *tried* to open it?"

"No," said Arlia. "It only took me two minutes to open it. I think someone knew what was in there and that's why they didn't try to get in."

"Can't argue with that," said Maddie. "And

remind me not to use those locks if I'm hiding anything from you."

Arlia blushed, although no one could tell. Her face was still red from all the chilli she'd eaten earlier on.

It's time for ...

Numbers!

with Arlia

If a simple lock just had the numbers 0 to 9 to choose from, then there are 10 options, right? 1 to 9 and also 0. So if there are 2 dials like this, then there are 100 different combinations possible (01 to 99 and 00). Or another way to work it out is 10 options (dial 1) × 10 options (dial 2) equals 100 possible combinations.

So how did Arlia know that 4 dials of 7 numbers had 2401 combinations? 7 options for the first dial, 7 for the next, and so on. In other words: 7 × 7 × 7 × 7 = 2401.

"All right, then," said Declan confidently, "so that just leaves ... what *does* that leave?" He stared helplessly at the whiteboard.

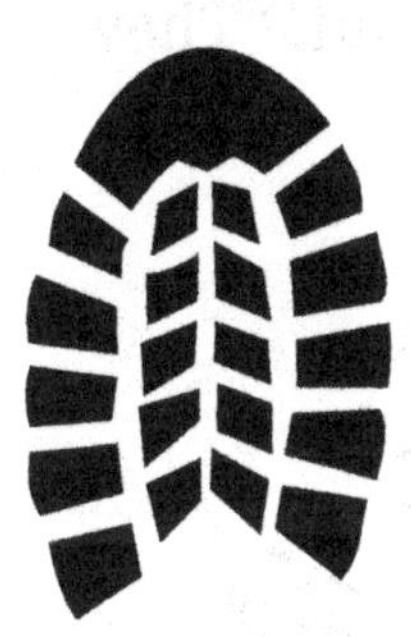

"There's the muddy shoe print on the paint tin you found," Sam offered. "And the exploded spray can that was near the fire."

They decided the shoe print was not the best clue. For starters, it seemed to be only half a shoe print (the front half). However, after measuring the front halves of all their shoes and the one on the paint tin, they figured it probably belonged to a size five shoe. Which meant someone about eleven to fifteen years old. Too young to have a car, as Arlia pointed out, so the driver must have had an accomplice.

As they considered the paint can, Declan began to chuckle to himself.

"What's so funny?" asked Sam.

"What do the spelling of *paint can* and the way we found this in the grass have in common?" He paused and then burst out, "They both start with P!"

With that, he was giggling uncontrollably. Sam and Arlia remembered the way Maddie had been high stepping through the grass with a horrified look on her face and both laughed as well. Maddie was not amused.

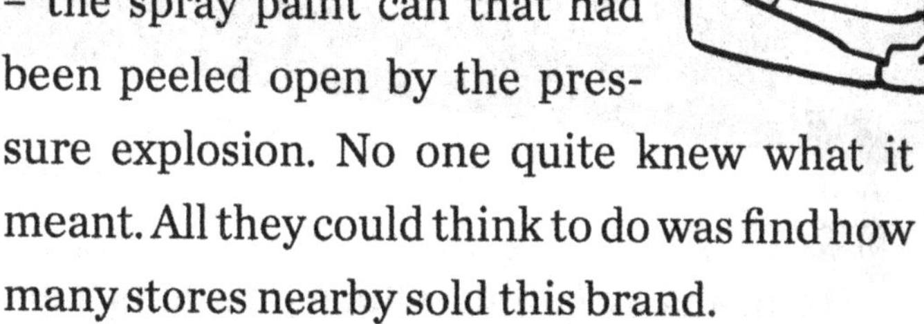

"I'm sorry," said Declan when he had finally calmed down. "Is it too soon?"

"It will *always* be too soon," said Maddie.

They turned their attention to their final piece of evidence – the spray paint can that had been peeled open by the pressure explosion. No one quite knew what it meant. All they could think to do was find how many stores nearby sold this brand.

"Hang on a minute!" said Declan. "I'm having a thought ... wait ... yes, got it! We need to buy a can of this paint and ensure it matches the graffiti. Just because we found the can nearby doesn't prove it was definitely used for the graffiti on the clubhouse. Not all reds are the same."

"There was red graffiti, and this was a red spray paint can, isn't that enough?" asked Sam. "How do you prove it's the same red? And we are not spraying more graffiti to see!"

"One word," said Declan. "Chromatography."

"Chroma-*what*?" asked Sam.

Chromatography

a method used to separate a mixture into its different parts. The mixture is dissolved in a fluid which is then passed through or over another material. The different parts of the mixture travel at different speeds, causing them to separate.

"It means we can see which pigments have been used to make this particular shade of red and compare them to a paint sample. But I'd need a can of that paint and a sample from the wall at the club. Sam, do you think you could get me access to that science lab at school again? I would do it myself, but I'm kind of grounded, on account of missing detention the other day. Weirdly, my parents don't mind if I skip school, so long as I do the work, but I can't skip detention apparently."

Everyone now had some tasks.

Sam was going to try to get the spray paint for Declan to look at. Maddie was going to try to create an image recognition program to use on the graffiti patterns around town, and Arlia offered to go and scrape a red paint sample from the soccer clubhouse.

They all agreed to meet in the science lab on Monday at lunchtime, assuming Mr Cobalt was okay with that.

CHAPTER 8

Change your passwords, people!

It was Monday and school had come around again all too fast. Not that the weekend actually goes any quicker than two school days, but it sure felt that way to Maddie. She woke up tired, but that had more to do with her late-night coding session on Sunday than the fact that it was Monday morning. She was actually a bit excited to show the others how well her program seemed to be working at finding graffiti matches.

When Maddie and Arlia arrived at the science lab, Sam looked deep in thought, while Declan was in the middle of some kind of chemical experiment that looked vaguely dangerous.

On the front desk sat a new can of spray paint that matched the exploded can they had found. Neither of the boys noticed that the girls had arrived, so Maddie cleared her throat and said, "You found the matching brand of spray paint, I see."

Sam snapped to attention. "What? Oh, the paint? Right. Yes, we have a new can, although *I* didn't exactly get it. Long story. Declan is getting everything ready to test this paint and some from the clubhouse. Arlia, did you get a chance to ...?"

Arlia dug through her school bag and produced a little snap lock bag containing some scrapings of red paint. "Will this do?" she asked, handing it to Declan.

"I don't know for sure yet, but I think so."

Declan took the paint samples, turned back around and went to work in the "fume hood". This is a bench that has a giant exhaust fan above it, and walls on the back and sides. On the front there was a pull-down, see-through window that went almost all the way to the bench, leaving just enough room for Declan's arms to go in and do his work. Even though he was not facing them, and seemed preoccupied with his paint matching, he continued talking.[4]

"So I got chatting to Mr Cobalt before. First time I had met him, but he seems to be a teacher who actually knows his stuff. Anyway, he figured I might need to use some pretty hard-core solvents to get this to work. He said he'd supervise, but I have no idea where he went. I mean, I could be up to anything in here for all he knows. If I were him, I wouldn't trust me."

"Then I guess it's lucky I'm not you," came the droll voice of Mr Cobalt.

Halfway through Declan's little speech, the teacher had entered silently through the internal door to the science lab. The others had seen him arrive, but Declan was busy in the fume hood and had his back turned.

"Umm, I'm sorry, Mr Cobalt," Declan stammered. "I didn't mean to say, it's just that ..."

It wasn't much of an apology, but Mr Cobalt waved it away. "Declan, is it? If that's a beaker of toluene you've got there, it really should be in the fume hood. Assuming everything else is okay, I'll get back to my lunch." Then he turned and left as silently as he had arrived.

Toluene

is a colourless liquid that is water insoluble (it doesn't mix with water). It is often used as a solvent (the stuff that does the dissolving) in paint thinner. It gives off smelly (and toxic!) fumes.

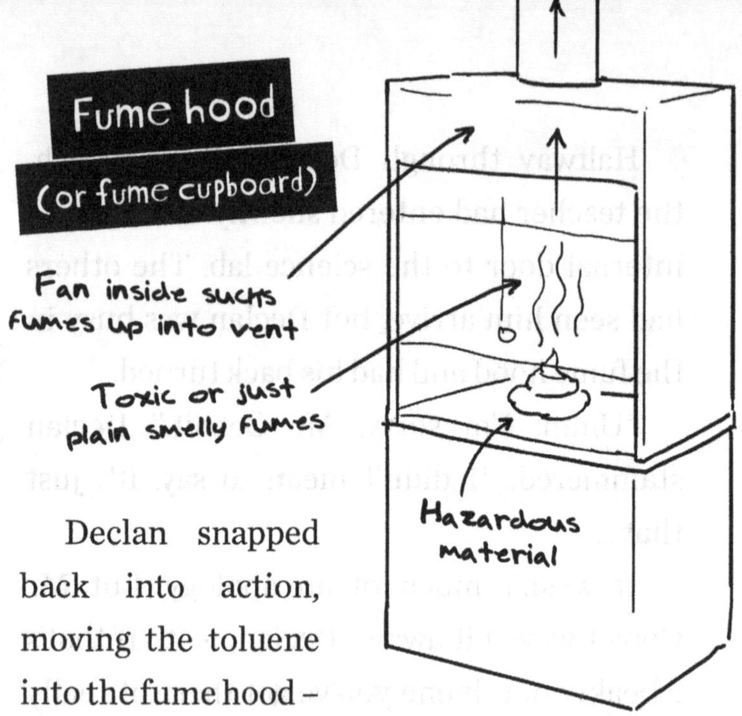

Declan snapped back into action, moving the toluene into the fume hood – it was a bit whiffy, after all. Arlia, Maddie and Sam stared after Mr Cobalt as they couldn't quite believe he had actually appeared.

"He's a strange one," whispered Maddie once she was sure the teacher was out of ear-shot.

"I guess he is a little odd," said Sam. "But he's been great with helping us. He even bought the can of spray paint."

"I thought you were buying it?" said Maddie.

Sam explained that he had gone to a few stores looking for the paint and finally found the matching brand, but when he went to buy it, they wouldn't sell it to him. Their policy was to only sell to adults. When he had explained all that to Mr Cobalt, and shown him the exploded can, the teacher offered to help.

"The thing is," said Sam, "I'm not convinced our exploded can was used the same night as the graffiti, anyway. It could have been used anytime, really. It might blow our whole idea out of the water. No pun intended."

Maddie considered his idea. "No doubt Declan's test will tell us if the paint matches up, but just in case ... Arlia, when that thing exploded, there would have been quite a *boom*, right?"

"For sure," replied Arlia. "It was like a small bomb."

Maddie grabbed her phone and quickly tapped in a number. "Hi, it's Maddie. I was hoping you could help me with something. I'm not sure if you can give out this information, but can you check the phone log and see if there were any reports of an explosion near the Brownleigh Football Club last Wednesday night." There was a pause. Finally, Maddie smiled, said, "Okay, thanks," and hung up.

"The police had two calls reporting a loud *boom* that night," she told the others.

"Great," said Sam uncertainly, mainly because he was still digesting the fact that Maddie had just called the police again. "Why do you have the phone number of someone from the police? Are they a relative or something?"

"That's another long story," said Maddie. "But in a nutshell, there was an incident, cyber-related ... mostly a misunderstanding, but I did *almost* get in quite a bit of trouble. Anyway, so now I know a couple of police officers, that's all."

They all wanted to know more, but Maddie had clearly said all she was going to say about the matter and changed the subject.

"Let me show you the cool image recognition program I put together."

She got out her laptop and fired it up. She warned them it didn't look all that great yet, because she hadn't bothered making it pretty and easy to use, but it was functional.

"I upload a graffiti image, like this one, select the area of interest, then tell it to try to find a match within a predefined geographic area. I used a 10-kilometre radius. Anyway, I don't need to run it again; I did it last night and this is what it spat out."

Maddie showed Sam and Arlia a map of their local area with all the successful graffiti matches as red dots. There was a distinct area to the north and east that had quite a bit of graffiti.

"My guess, and it's just a guess, is that the perps likely live or work around that area."

"You know what else is interesting?" asked Sam. "The store where that paint comes from is right here, on the edge of the hot zone."

Declan had not been listening to any of this breaking news, but had some of his own as he ran over clutching two strips with red and orange streaks along their length. "Look what I found!" he said.

"The paints match?" said Arlia.

Declan looked a little crestfallen. "How

did you know? Have you analysed chromatograms before?"

"Oh, no, it's just that ... well, I suppose it's just a guess really."

Declan nodded. "A guess is a good start, but we need proof, right? And I have it!" He laid the twin strips on the bench and pointed out the features as he went. "This one is made from the paint sample scraped from the wall. You can see the individual pigments separate as they are drawn upwards and that this red paint actually contains some orange and purple too. And when you compare it to the paint from the spray can, you find exactly the same pigment mix. In other words, it's the same red."

Now that Declan had filled them in on his breakthrough, Sam explained what they had discovered, and they made plans to meet at the hardware store that afternoon.

A few hours later, Maddie and Declan waited outside the hardware store while Sam talked to the sales assistant inside. It wasn't long before Sam joined them on the pavement.

"He said no."

"Did you explain what it was all about? You know, that it's for a good cause and all that?" Declan asked.

"Yep, and he still said no. I don't think the guy I spoke to owns the store – he sure doesn't want to be there today, and didn't want to be dealing with me."

"Now what?" asked Maddie.

Sam frowned. He did have a "Plan B", but he would need both Declan's and Maddie's help to execute it. He quickly explained his idea.

This time Maddie went into the shop and walked straight up to the counter. She asked a few simple questions about pipes, casually dumping her bag and phone on the counter. The staff member scratched his head, then took her to the taps and spouts aisle to show her, as it was easier than explaining. As soon as they had left, Declan headed up to the counter. He asked the other sales person how much copper sulphate they had in stock. It was a strange question and he knew it, but it was all he could think of. He wasn't very good at covert operations. Once the staff member had looked it up for him on the computer, he went and bought some (he needed it anyway) and left. After Declan had left, Maddie returned to the counter and grabbed her phone and bag.

"Thanks anyway for your help," she said.

Sam and Declan were already waiting in the carpark when Maddie exited the store.

"Time to see if that worked," she said. She held out her phone and played the most recent video. The camera had started recording in video mode before she entered the store, so it was still recording when she had carefully placed it just over the counter edge, with the camera looking straight down at the store's computer keyboard. As the video played, they listened to Maddie ask for help, then go, then Declan ask for help. It was about now that fingers appeared in the video, typing a password on the computer to log in to the store inventory. "Aha!" said Sam out loud. Maddie smiled

and furiously went to work on her laptop to see if this long shot might pay off.

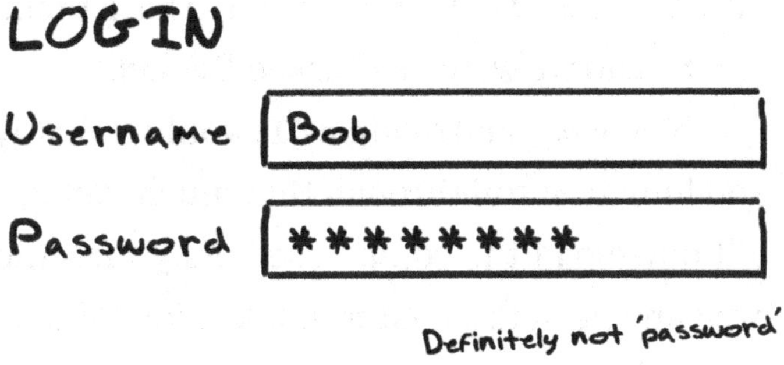

LOGIN

Username Bob

Password *********

Definitely not 'password'

"We're not there yet," she said, not wanting to crush their hopes but trying to be realistic all the same. "That might have just been the staff password for the inventory, but I suspect that they use one password for all their systems – most people and companies do – it's just easier. Well ... look at that. We're in! Sam, this just might work. But we still have to hope they allow remote access to their security camera log files. Which isn't unusual I guess, you can check most CCTV cameras remotely these days. So with any luck ... yep, it worked! People, you gotta change your passwords." She had said the last part to herself, but Declan and Sam both decided to do exactly that in case Maddie ever tried to hack them.

"So can we watch it?" asked Declan.

"Not now," said Maddie. "It would take way too long to scroll through that much footage. I'll download the compressed daily files and we can check them later. Looks like it'll take about five minutes."

"Okay," said Sam, "But ... is this ... you know, legal?"

Maddie thought for a while before replying. "I guess it's a grey area. Which is probably not great for me given what happened last year. So ... next question."

They decided instead to talk about why Declan had bought copper sulphate. (In case you're wondering, it was mainly for his dad to use in their pool. But Declan also hoped to try to grow a big blue copper sulphate crystal, as well.)

If you've ever owned a swimming pool, one thing you need to be careful about is that the water doesn't turn green or brown. This can happen if algae grow in there. Algae are organisms that live in water, growing and multiplying when there's a lot of food and sunlight around. (Seaweed is a type of algae.) One common way to deal with problem algae is to use an algaecide (that is, something that kills algae). Copper sulphate is an ingredient in many pool algaecides, and even though you use it in very tiny amounts, it can kill all the algae in there.

But there can be a side effect.

Green hair.

If there is copper in the pool water, it can get into a swimmer's hair and stick to it. The copper then oxidises and turns a green colour (when iron oxidises it turns brown, and we call it rust). As a result of the copper turning green, any light-coloured hair (like blonde hair) can take on a green-ish tinge too.

CHAPTER 9

The headless man has a name!

That night, Maddie messaged the others to let them know she'd assigned each of them a couple of days of the store's CCTV video footage to scroll through. It was all digital, which made it easier, although there were four cameras throughout the store, all recording simultaneously. The sheer volume of video blew out the file sizes so she'd had to downgrade it to a lower resolution in order to upload it all. Maddie suggested they concentrate

CCTV

stands for 'closed circuit television'. It is most commonly used for security surveillance. A week's worth of video footage from a modern CCTV system would be about 150 gigabytes!

on camera 1, which was at the sales counter, and camera 4, which showed the aisle that had the spray paint section at the far end. They should look for anyone picking up or buying spray paint and note the day and time. They could then meet at school and check out any potentially interesting moments on the high-res original on Maddie's hard drive. It'd be much easier to take snapshots or zoom in and get clearer images that way.

Given the slightly naughty (and possibly illegal) way they'd obtained the video, they thought it better not to sit outside where people might wander over and ask what they were doing. So they trudged up to the science block to see if Mr Cobalt would let them use Room 312 again.

"There's a group already in there," said Arlia, as she peered in the window.

"I presume you want to use this room again."

Arlia jumped. Mr Cobalt had appeared behind them silently.

"As you can see, it's busy on Tuesdays," he went on. "I'm sure you could squeeze in a back corner, but then you'd have to tell everyone you went to *science club*."

As he said this, Maddie felt like he was staring straight at her. How did he know about her objection to clubs?

Sam spoke up. "Thanks for the offer, Mr Cobalt, it's just that today, it's probably best if we don't do our work ... around a lot of people."

"I see," said Mr Cobalt, after a moment. Although exactly *what* he saw wasn't clear, because Sam's speech made very little sense, unless you already knew what he was talking about. "Follow me then."

Mr Cobalt led them into the lab and then through the internal door that led to the preparation lab. Only Mr Cobalt and the lab technician were allowed in this room. There were shelves stacked with chemicals arranged in alphabetical order, beakers, flasks and all manner of interesting equipment. There was a big yellow cupboard labelled "SOLVENTS", three different sets of scientific scales, and an enormous sink. Sitting on the sink was a large covered tub with the words "ACID BATH" written on the side and a "WARNING: CORROSIVE!" sticker on it. There was also a strange smell.

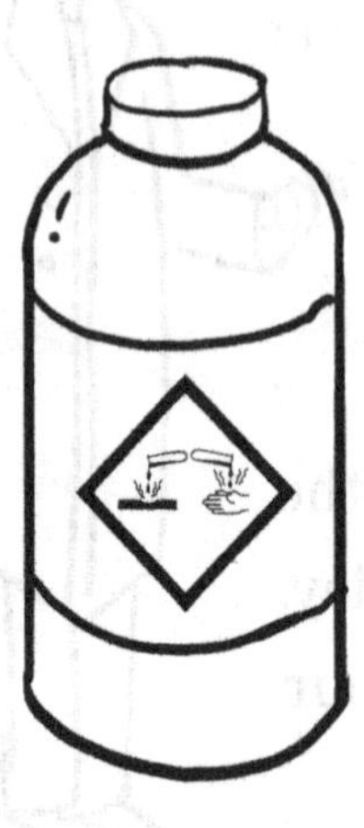

Be careful if you see the corrosive warning

"You can sit here," said Mr

Cobalt, gesturing to a small table in the middle. "I'd better go and rescue Mrs Schumann before she's completely overcome by student enthusiasm." And with that he headed back towards the noisy science club next door. Just before he closed the door, and without looking at any of them in particular, he said, "Don't touch anything outside of that desk."

"He didn't mean me, did he?" asked Declan, although he knew the answer already. "I guess I'm not very good at first impressions. Or second ones sometimes ..."

Maddie got out her laptop and they set to work. First, they reviewed the days Declan had been assigned, skipping straight to the times of interest he had written down.

"Go to Sunday 10 am," he said, and Maddie

did just that. "Okay, play and watch, this is hilarious."

They played the video and watched as two young children raced around the store pushing empty mini-trolleys. Their frazzled mother was trying to ignore them as she chose light switches on camera 3. "Here it comes ..." said Declan excitedly. And sure enough, the two kids racing mini-trolleys swung around the end of the same aisle but in different directions and crashed into each other. Declan and Sam laughed. Arlia winced, wondering if the kids had hurt themselves. Maddie just stared.

"It's okay, they're fine. I watched the rest, they got in trouble from their mum. Play it again, Maddie, it's so good."

"Don't get me wrong, I normally find this kind of thing hilarious," she said drily. "But we have twenty-five minutes left to look for some clues on this footage, so can we save the 'Fail' video moments for some other time?"

She was right and they all knew it, even though they would have loved to have seen that crash again.

Declan read out some other times of interest and they began searching.

On the footage from Monday they saw Mr Cobalt come in and buy the paint he had given them to test, and they even saw themselves go in that afternoon. Two other people had bought spray paint that day and they did their best to capture and save a still-frame picture of them.

Even though it had been fun to spot themselves and Mr Cobalt in the store, it made more sense to start from the day of the vandalism attack and work backwards. After all, that was most likely when the paint was bought, assuming it was bought from this store.

Almost instantly, they found something a little curious. A man in jeans and a grubby work shirt and a boy about their age had come in on the Tuesday afternoon and grabbed a couple of cans of spray paint. Unfortunately, they couldn't get a good image from camera 4, because it was at the end of the aisle, but they could see the pair walk off towards the sales counter. Strangely though, when the man and boy reappeared at the front of the store, they

no longer had the spray paint cans, and were instead buying a small plant.

"I bet you they're nicking the paint," Maddie said. "It'll be in the kid's school backpack. The plant is just a diversion."

They checked the other cameras and she was right: up the back near the BBQs, the man had quietly slipped two cans of spray paint into the boy's backpack.

"So how do we find out who they are?" asked Arlia.

They all turned back to the footage. Camera 1 filmed the sales counter and should have been their best bet, but unfortunately the camera was pointed too low and cut off the heads of the adult customers. So all they could see was a headless man and a boy with his back turned. Not great.

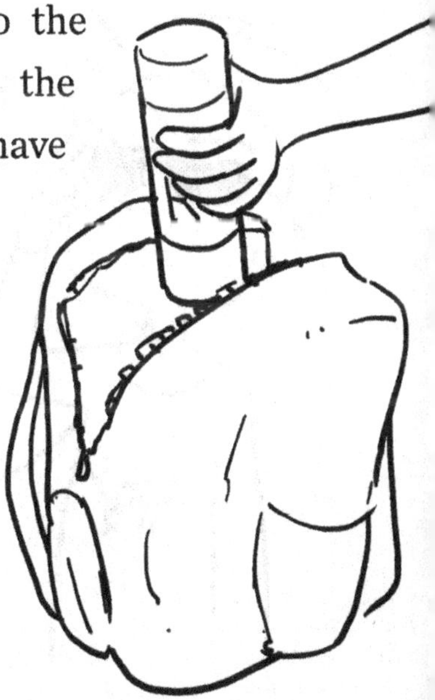

Thankfully, the boy turned around as the pair went to leave and they saw his face.

"I know him!" said Sam, pointing at the screen. "At least, I know his face. I never forget a face, but I'm not so good with names. He used to play soccer at the club, a year younger than me ... Come on, brain ... Alfie, his name is Alfie!"

It's ...

Face time!

with Sam

We humans are pretty good at recognising faces. When we see someone familiar (a friend, a relative or a movie star) we know who it is just by looking at their face. By the time you're an adult, the number of faces you can recognise is well into the thousands. And what's more, our brain copes with things like new hairstyles, glasses, beards, even seeing someone at a weird angle in dim light.

But we can't remember everyone, right? Well maybe. There are people who *do* remember almost every face they see, and scientists call them "super-recognisers". And at the other end are people who can barely remember a face, even of people they know well.

It turns out we are not the only ones who can recognise human faces. Dogs are pretty good, cats not so good. Some birds and fish can recognise familiar human faces. And of course computers can do it. Some programs are amazing at facial recognition, but for the moment at least, humans still win if the conditions are not ideal (like at night, or side on).

"Alfie who?" asked Maddie, getting ready to do a search on her computer. "What's his last name?"

Sam threw up his arms. "I don't know," he admitted.

Luckily Maddie had enough to go on. She started trawling through the website archives of the Brownleigh Football Club for photos, player names in teams, anything. Soon she found him.

"Alfie Stenson?" she asked.

"Alfie Stenson!" Sam confirmed, as if he'd known it all along.

They had unravelled one mystery, but another still remained. Who was the headless, grubby man with Alfie? Arlia suggested they were relatives. Maddie again checked the club archives, this time for any Stensons at

all – and one came up. He only played a year, was nine years older than Alfie, and looked like Alfie's brother. His name was Nick.

"So how do we track down Nick or Alfie?" asked Sam.

"Same way you track down anyone these days," said Maddie, already typing.

"Social media!" said Declan. It was good he said it out loud because Sam thought the answer was Wikipedia and Arlia was thinking newspapers.

Within a matter of minutes, Maddie had found out plenty about Nick Stenson – parties he'd been to and friends he had. There were also a few nice family pictures of him and Alfie, lots of shared photos and articles about cars and, perhaps most importantly, a picture of him at work. He was a mechan-

ic, although exactly where was not so clear. Sadly, the metadata, including the geotag, had been stripped off when the work photo had been uploaded, so Maddie couldn't figure out where it was taken. This mystified her because most people had no idea how to turn off the geotagging on their phones. As a result they often uploaded their photos with it embedded, making it very easy to find the location, if you knew how. But even without a location, it felt like a win, a big step towards catching the perps.

It's time for ...

Data Wrangling!

with Maddie

In the old days, when photos had to be developed from film, people would often write things on the back of the printed photo, like people's names, the date and the location. In the digital age, if you take a photo with a smartphone (or smart camera), the chances are there's something called "metadata" attached to the picture. You don't normally see it, but it's usually there and it includes a bunch of things about the photo such as camera type, date, time, GPS coordinates and even altitude! Which is great if you have a bad memory for exactly where a holiday snap was taken. But not so good if you are a celebrity on a secret holiday who has posted a picture of something, like a plate of food. If the photo has a geotag, suddenly a lot of people might know exactly where you are eating!

With lunchtime almost over, they packed up the computer and headed out via the big science lab. The science club were busily cleaning up from their meeting.

"No food today?" Declan asked Sam. He had forgotten his lunch and his stomach rumbled.

"Ah, I forgot to tell Dan where I'd be," said Sam. "Still, I'm kind of surprised he didn't find us. He's good at finding things, it's like his super power."

As they exited the science block, they ran into the very person they had just been talking about.

"Sorry, it's all gone," Dan said, although he didn't look sorry. "I looked for you in Room 312, but the teacher with the science club wouldn't let me in with food, so my mates and I ate it."

"Don't worry about it," said Sam. "Thanks for trying."

"What was it today?" asked Declan eagerly. "Was it delicious?"

Dan just smiled. "I'm not sure how to describe it to you, but it was *really* good."

Maddie was hungry too, but seeing Dan had given her an idea. She grabbed her phone, brought up the picture of Nick outside his workshop and showed it to Sam's little brother to see if he knew where it was. You couldn't see much of the building, but this kid had super powers, so it was worth a shot.

"That's the mechanic attached to the service station on Gibson Street, I think."

That was good enough for the rest of them – they now had a place to check out that afternoon.

Super Dan

Bringing the banh mi

(if you don't know what a banh mi is, it's delicious)

CHAPTER 10

We are not the police?

"Well, that's the place all right," whispered Sam as he held up the image on Maddie's phone and compared it to the real thing. He didn't really need to whisper – they were on the other side of a busy road from the service station – but he felt it added to the atmosphere.

"Yep, that's it," agreed Declan. "So, now what? We go over there and arrest him?"

"Um, I'm pretty sure we can't do that," said Arlia. "We do have a convincing story that implicates him and maybe his brother, but we need more."

"Also," added Maddie, "we are *not* the police."

"Oh, no! I think he's seen us," hissed Declan, standing on his toes and holding a pair binoculars.

The others ignored Declan's panic and squinted at the figure that had emerged from the workshop across the road. It certainly looked like Nick, but there was no chance he would recognise them. He didn't know who they were, or that they had been investigating

him. Once Sam explained this to Declan, he calmed down and began to survey the scene again with his binoculars.

“Okay, here’s the plan,” said Sam. “Let’s all walk over there. Arlia and I will talk to Nick about something, keep him distracted, and then take a closer look inside the workshop. Meanwhile, Declan, you check around the back and Maddie, you set up near the shop so we can send any pictures or video straight to you, in case he busts us. Which he won't. But at least we'll get to keep the evidence."

They crossed the road and split up. Sam and Arlia went into the workshop, which was largely empty and looked like it was about to be closed up for the day. Nick soon spotted them.

Unfortunately, now it was Sam's turn to panic. He searched around for something to say. "Oh, hi, Nick. I was just wondering if you had any ... you know, spark plugs?"

Nick looked puzzled. "Okay, um, what sort of car are the plugs for? And how do you know my name? Have we met?"

Sam went blank. Why had he said Nick's name?

Thankfully Arlia jumped in. "Your name's on your shirt," she said matter-of-factly.

"Oh yeah, that's right. I'm always forgetting that. It's a new shirt. Now, what sort of car did you say?" He was talking to Sam again, who was about to have his second brain freeze.

"Ah, it's a diesel," said Sam.

"I meant what *make* of car is it?" said Nick. "And are you sure you want spark plugs for a diesel?"

"*Glow* plugs," chimed in Arlia, saving Sam for the second time in less than a minute. "He meant glow plugs. For an old VW Golf."

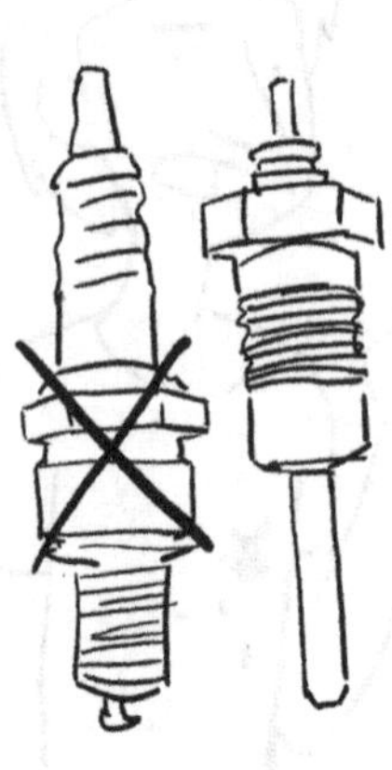

"Right. Got it." Nick seemed relieved to finally understand. "I might be able to help there. Follow me out back."

While Sam and Nick headed out the back door, Arlia stayed behind and quickly began scouring the workshop for clues.

Engines (petrol vs diesel)

Most cars and trucks need either petrol or diesel to make them go. These are two very different types of fuel, which means the engines that use them are also very different. In both cases the fuel is burnt inside the engine (this is why they're known as internal combustion engines), and this explosive reaction is harnessed to make the vehicle move. In a petrol engine, a little of the petrol is mixed with air then squashed in a cylinder by a piston until finally a spark (from the spark plug) ignites the mixture, turning a shaft which eventually moves the wheels, making the car go. In a diesel engine, there's no spark to make the fire. Instead, the diesel is mixed with air that has been squashed so much that the heat and pressure causes the fuel to ignite and turn the engine. However, if a diesel engine is cold, it may need a little help. Inside the engine are glow plugs (metal prongs that get so hot they glow), and they're used to help heat the diesel-air mixture to combustion point.

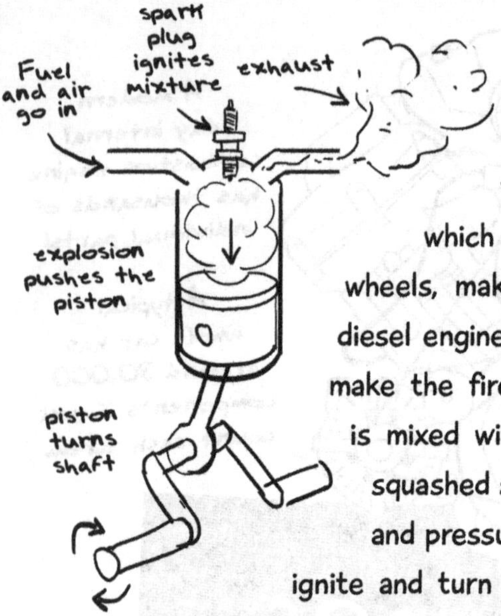

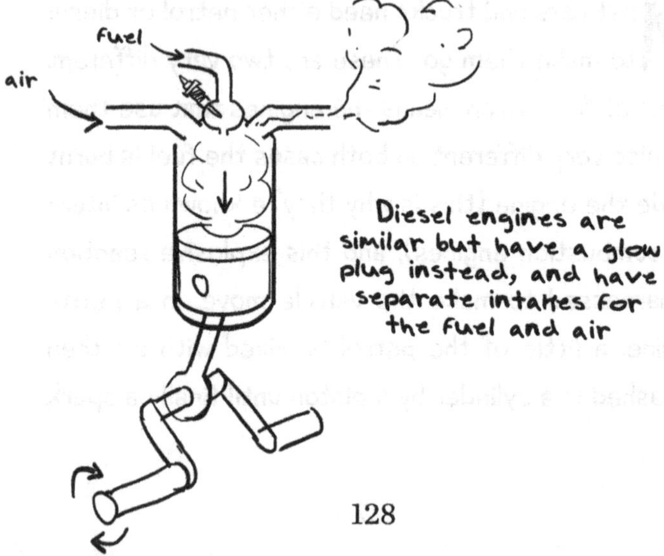

While all this was happening, Declan had struck gold. As soon as he walked around the back of the workshop, he noticed the hotted-up car with a bit of mud up the side. He checked the tyre patterns and then called Maddie using a walkie-talkie app on his phone. Maddie didn't like the app, but it made Declan feel more like a spy, so she went with it.

"Maddie, I think I've found the car that tore up the soccer oval. Over ... I mean, not over. Can you please send me the tyre track photos? Over, again."

Declan was talking in very hushed tones.

Maddie's reply was not so hushed. "Right, I've sent one. And I'm not saying 'over'."

"You just did," said Declan, suppressing a laugh. "Over."

Declan compared the photo from the soccer field with the tyre of the car he was crouching behind. It looked like a pretty solid match.

"Maddie, I think we have a match. I'm going to read out the number plate. Can you run a search on it? Over."

"No, I cannot run a search on a number plate!" came the reply crackling through the phone. "Well, not easily, and it's illegal. This is no grey area, it's black and white. Just take a photo and come back over."

"Ha! You said 'over' again! Right, I'm taking the photo now and ... uh oh, someone's coming."

Declan was interrupted by Sam and Nick looking for glow plugs. Nick saw Declan taking a photo of his car and marched straight over to him. "What are you doing?" he growled.

"Taking a photo?" replied Declan, his voice wavering.

"Well, why are you doing it from that

angle?" Nick's face broke into a smile. "Come and take one from the front, mate. With the sun this low, you need to get it from the front. She's a beauty, eh? I did her up myself."

Relieved, Declan dutifully took a couple of pictures from the front, including one with Nick posing next to the car, giving the thumbs-up. Then he thanked Nick and went to find Maddie.

The unexpected photo shoot had given Arlia a little extra time to snoop about and take a couple of shots, but before long Sam and Nick were back. Thankfully Nick hadn't found any suitable glow plugs, so they didn't have to keep up their charade. Just as they were about to leave, Arlia noticed Nick's jeans.

"Hey, how did you get those red marks on your pants?" As soon as the words were out of her mouth, she realised it sounded like an accusation. So she quickly switched to a very high, girly voice and added, "You know, it's for, like, my fashion blog. Can I take a photo? That is sooo on trend."

Nick seemed confused but agreed to pose for his second photo in two minutes. Then he shook his head as if in disbelief and went about locking up for the day.

By the time they had left and were a block away, Declan finally stopped looking over his shoulder to make sure Nick wasn't following them.

Maddie pulled up the photos and flicked through them. The car tyres seem to match the tracks in the field. The mud up the side of the car was a bonus. There was also a cheesy selfie of Declan with the car behind him, obviously taken before Nick had come out. Maddie rolled her eyes and swiftly hit the delete key before moving on.

"Hey, you just deleted that last one," said Declan.

"Did I? Oops, I'm not very good with computers," she replied, smirking. Then came the photos Arlia had taken in the workshop while Nick and Sam were out the back. First there was a flat-bladed screwdriver, and then a close-up of the end of the same screwdriver.

"You think that could be what they used to lever open the door at the club?" ask Sam.

"Maybe," said Arlia. "It looks the right size, and of course it was in his workshop."

"But surely there are loads of screwdrivers in any mechanic's workshop," said Sam.

"Yeah, lots," replied Arlia. "But most of them have a Phillips head. You know, the sort with the star shape? Mechanics don't have as many flat-headed screwdrivers because cars don't really have slotted head screws. You can thank car manufacturers for that."

Have you ever noticed there are two main types of screws? The slot-head screw (with a single slot across the top), and the Phillips head screw (with a cross on the top). The slot and the cross are for screwdrivers to fit into and turn the screws.

The slot-head screw was around first, but in the 1930s an engineer named John Thompson came up with this new cross-head design. But nobody really seemed to want it. So he sold the idea to Henry F. Phillips, who refined it and got the manufacturing industry interested. Car makers (among others) loved it, because it made manufacturing quicker and easier. Its popularity spread like wildfire, and the screw is still named after Henry Phillips. These days there are over 20 different screw designs used for various things, but Mr Phillips' design is still a winner.

Nobody knew what to say to that, so they just nodded in agreement and moved on. There were a couple of photos of the inside of the workshop that Maddie had taken in case they wanted to look at something a bit closer later on. There was also a close-up of a pair of giant pliers.

"Those are bolt cutters," said Arlia. "Really big bolt cutters."

Exhibit A?

"Hmm, okay," said Maddie, trying to see how this might link to their case.

"I don't think the bolt cutters have anything to do with the stuff at the soccer club," Arlia explained. "I just thought they were a really big pair of bolt cutters for a mechanic's workshop to have. I'm not sure what they'd use them for, actually."

The last photos were of the jeans with the red speckles around the ends of the legs.

"He wouldn't have got that paint on his jeans doing the graffiti, would he?" said Sam.

"No, I don't think so ..." replied Arlia.

Declan and Maddie both had the realisation at the same time. "The red exploding can!"

"Yeah, that's what I figured," said Arlia. "And given how close he must have been standing to the can when it went *kaboom,* he's lucky he only got a bit of paint on his jeans. He could've ended up in hospital."

Exhibit B?

The afternoon, and the new photos, only served to cement what they already thought. The evidence seemed to point towards Nick and Alfie. They all agreed it was time to go to the police and see what they could do. But which one of them should go? They were all proud of their detective work, but no one particularly wanted to go into a police station. What if the first person they spoke to just told them to "go home" and "stop trying to do an adult's job"? Arlia told the others she was too nervous, and Declan said he was worried he might confess to a crime he hadn't committed. In the end they decided that Maddie and Sam should do it together. They'd go right before school tomorrow.

CHAPTER 11

It's a team?

The cake sitting on the ping-pong table was amazing. It had smooth chocolate icing with curls of actual chocolate on top. It looked good enough to have come from a cake shop, but Arlia assured Declan she had made it herself. Her two strengths were baking and Newtonian physics. An odd combination, but it didn't bother her.

The door opened and Maddie strode in, dumping her bag on the nearest chair before collapsing into a large beanbag.

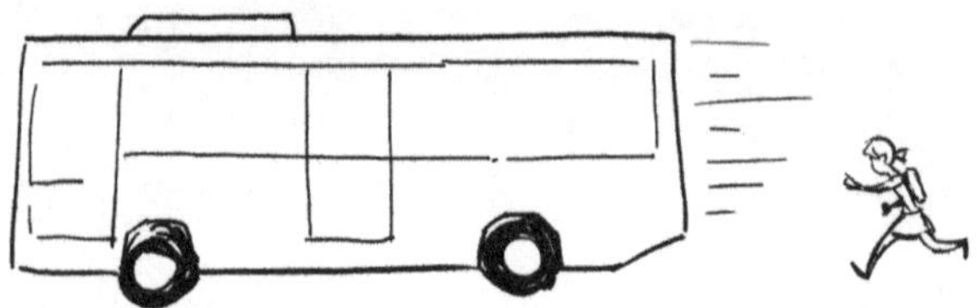

"Missed the bus, so I had to walk before catching a different bus. I wish they could just put them all on some app in real time – it would make life so much easier." Arlia and Declan nodded politely, but they weren't really interested in fixing the public transport network. They had been hanging out to see how things went with the police that morning. Sam was supposed to be here by now too, but soccer practice had made him late.

"So ..." said Declan. "How did it go?"

"How did what go?" asked Maddie, innocently.

Just then Sam burst in, out of breath and still wearing his bike helmet. "Guess who I just saw down at the soccer club, starting to paint over all the graffiti?"

Maddie sighed. She had been hoping to string out the anticipation a little longer.

Arlia was about to reply when Declan jumped in. "What? Really? Already? They made Nick paint over the mess?"

"Nick *and* Alfie," said Sam. "I didn't want to get too close in case Nick saw me and worked out I had something to do with it." They all turned to Maddie, who clearly knew the full story.

"All right," she said at last. "We went to the police station this morning as planned and laid out all the evidence we'd collected. They seemed to take us seriously. But that was it, so we left."

"That was it?" cried Declan.

"For this morning, at least," continued Maddie, really milking it. "I got a call after school asking if we could come in again. Sam had soccer, but I went. The senior sergeant just wanted to let us know they had confronted the boys with some of the evidence and they had confessed. Apparently it had been Nick's idea, but Alfie idolises his brother and does whatever he says. Basically it was like we thought. They stole the paints that afternoon, then at dusk drove down to the field and Nick began showing off to Alfie, hooning around the field in his car. Then they went up to the clubhouse to graffiti it. Alfie tried to get in that window and then Nick forced the door with a screwdriver from his work. Apparently, he needed money, but he also had a grudge against the club because of something that happened when he played there. Afterwards

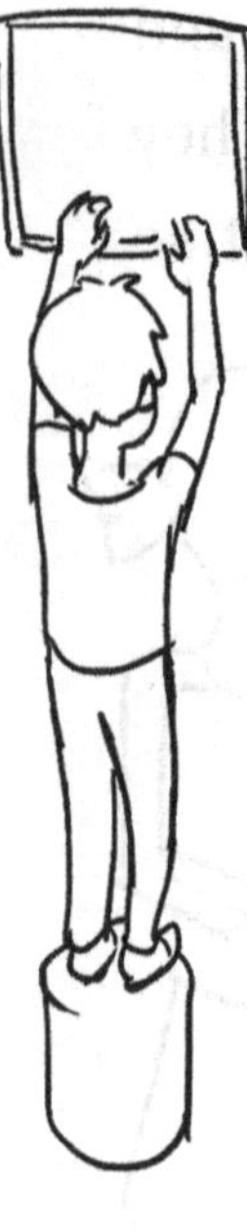

they both had a little campfire down near the creek, and Nick dropped an empty can on the fire as a joke. He had no idea it would explode. Apparently his ears still hurt! He and Alfie offered to repaint the clubhouse as a kind of peace offering, and the hardware store is supplying the paint because they felt bad about their spray cans being used for graffiti. The store has also been advised to change their system password. And I nearly got barred from computer access for a while, for the whole 'grey area' thing. But I got a lecture instead."

"Wow, it all makes sense now," said Sam, almost to himself. He realised the others were staring at him. "Oh, it's just that I remember hearing a story about a goalkeeper a few years back in one of the older sides. Apparently, he was really good, but in a grand final he scored an own goal, his team lost, and he never played again. I think some people blamed him for the loss. And I'm pretty sure it was Nick. I think that might be why it all happened. And the stupid thing is, it wasn't his fault, it should never have been a goal."

"How come?" asked Arlia.

"It was really wet and muddy that day. Nick was goalkeeper and he went to take a goal kick, slipped, missed the ball entirely with his foot and sat on it instead, sending it backwards into the net."

"Oh no," said Declan. "That would have made an epic fail video."

"Yeah, it would have looked

pretty funny," agreed Sam, "but it should never have been a goal. A goal kick has to leave the eighteen-yard box to be in play. The ref got it wrong. I think it should have just been a corner kick after his slip-up."

Arlia nodded, although she had no idea what the difference between a goal kick and a corner kick was.

"But there's more," Sam went on. "This afternoon I overheard a conversation after training while I was getting changed. The head coach of the adult team seemed to recognise someone he hadn't seen in a while. He told him to come down and try out, said they could do with someone of his talent. The guy replied that he'd think about it. I think it was Nick."

They sat there for a while, soaking it in. They had just helped solve a crime. They were heroes. And, more importantly, they were heroes with cake.

"Let's celebrate," said Sam as he cut the cake. He handed each of them a slice and there was silence as they enjoyed the rich, chocolatey treat.

Maddie spoke first. "This is really good cake, Arls."

Arlia grinned. It was the first time anyone had given her a nickname and it made her go a bit tingly.

"Actually, while we're in a celebratory mood," began Declan, "I've got something I'd like to show you all. I've been working on this for a while ..." He rummaged under the table and pulled out a box.

"You know how I said we needed a name ... well, I figured that now we've had our first success, 'caught our first perp' so to speak, we should all have business cards and shirts. So I had some made up."

The others were intrigued, and a little confused. Declan handed around the business cards.

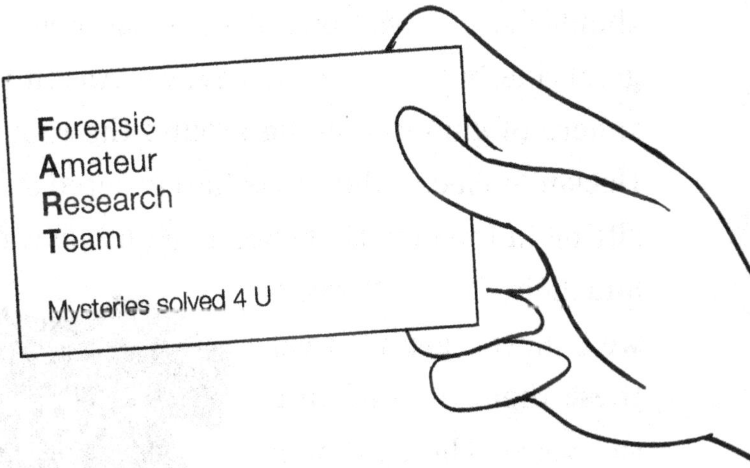

"But Declan," began Maddie, "I don't want to get all negative here, but I don't think we can do this again. Don't get me wrong, I had fun, and I'm glad Nick and Alfie got caught. But the police officer today wasn't exactly full of gratitude. I pretty much got an official warning and was told to leave police work to the police. If we continue, it could be dangerous or something. So, yeah, I think that's it. It's kind of ... over."

Everyone was quiet as the reality of Maddie's words sunk in. Maybe they had just got lucky with their first "case", maybe they should have stayed out of it. It had been a great ride, but it seemed it *was* over. An atmosphere of glumness hung around the room. Declan looked at the shirts he'd ordered still sitting in the box. He fished one out anyway and held it up. "I guess we'll never get to wear these then," he said in a sad voice. The shirt was a copy of an American SWAT team shirt, but instead of S.W.A.T. in big

white writing on the front of a black shirt, this one read F.A.R.T.

The real SWAT

Sure you can use a swat to kill a fly, but if you use a SWAT team, you are getting into much more dangerous territory. Originating in the United States, S.W.A.T. stands for "Special Weapons And Tactics" and they are a unit of the police force that operates more like the army. SWAT teams are usually heavily armed, have a lot of body armour and shields and are used during dangerous raids or to stop riots. Because they don't wear a police uniform, they instead have SWAT on their outfits so they can be readily identified.

Declan was still staring sadly at the shirt when Maddie answered her phone.

"Hello. Oh, yes, that's me ... okay ... really? Um, yeah, sure."

It was always hard to read Maddie's voice but she sounded almost upbeat.

"So that was the chief forensic officer," she explained. "She was just given all the evidence we collected and told the story of where it came from. Apparently she was a little bit impressed. And she outranks the senior sergeant who told me off earlier."

The others waited eagerly to hear more, but Maddie simply popped the last bit of cake into her mouth and announced she had a mountain of homework to do.

"So ... does this mean we're back in business?" Declan asked.

Maddie was already halfway out the door when she

Maddie's homework

replied, "Yes, Dec, we are. But the shirts might be a bit much."

Had Maddie turned around she would have seen Declan punch the air in victory, then put on a shirt and dance a strange jig while Sam and Arlia laughed. But the door had shut, and now that she was safely outside and alone, she allowed herself a big smile.

THE END

The F.A.R.T. will return ...

ENDNOTES

1. Cracking the code

To crack the code, Arlia uses the alphabet key:

1 = A, 2 = B, 3 = C,
and so on.

The first sum on the note was 1 + 3 = 8. The correct answer to the sum is 4, which meant that it was wrong by 4, so maybe 4 held the key? Adding 4 to the sum (e.g. 1 + 3 + 4 = 8) made it correct, so maybe each of the numbers in the top line needed to have 4 added to them.

So instead of "14, 11, 11, 9 312", the top line now became:

18, 15, 15, 13 316

This was better! Using her alphabet code key this now half made sense:

"ROOM CAF".

The second line was quickly decoded too. The sum became correct by subtracting 5 (e.g. 6 + 4 – 5 = 5), so Arlia subtracted 5 from each of the numbers in the second line, and then used her alphabet key.

15, 14, 5 15, 3, 12, 15, 3, 11 → ONE O'CLOCK

2. Elephant's Toothpaste Experiment

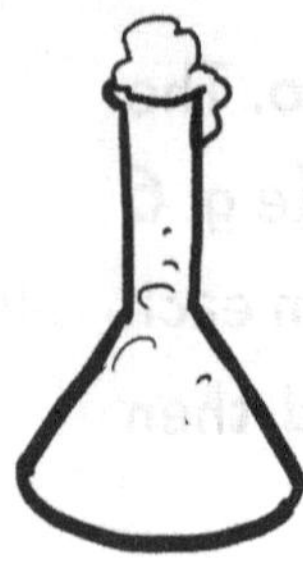

Here is the home-friendly version of the Elephant's Toothpaste Experiment (not Declan's version that exploded all over the science lab – but make sure the area is able to be cleaned easily and always make sure an adult is nearby in case of an emergency!!)

Stuff you need

- 120 ml 6 per cent peroxide
- 1 sachet of yeast
- food colour
- detergent
- 600 ml empty soft drink bottle

How to do it

- Mix the yeast with 4 tablespoons of warm water in a cup, and leave aside for 10 minutes.
- Measure the peroxide into the empty bottle, add a small squeeze of detergent and swirl.
- Dribble a few drops of different food colours down the inside of the bottle.
- Lastly, add the yeast mixture and wait for the foam to roam!

What's going on?

Peroxide is like water with some extra oxygen crammed in there. The chemical formula for water is H_2O, but peroxide is H_2O_2, and adding in this extra oxygen makes it unstable. Peroxide is happy to lose the extra oxygen and just go back to being water. To speed that up, you can use a catalyst. In this case it is an enzyme (or biological chemical) called *catalase* and it is made by the yeast. The catalase helps pull apart the peroxide, and the oxygen gas being released is trapped in the detergent making bubbles. The steam happens because heat is released when the peroxide splits into water and oxygen. The food colour was just for fun!

3. Recipe – Banh Xeo
(Saigon Sizzlers or Vietnamese Pancakes)

Ingredients

- Pancakes
- 200 g rice flour
- 300 ml coconut milk
- 100 ml water
- 1 teaspoon ground turmeric
- Shallots (spring onions)
- Pak choy or lettuce
- Onions, bean sprouts
- Meat (cut up squid/pork belly/shrimp/chicken)

Before you start cooking, make sure there's an adult close by in case of an emergency!

Pancake batter

Mix the flour, coconut milk, water and turmeric until it's a smooth, gloopy liquid. Add some finely sliced shallots and a pinch of salt. Leave for 30 minutes while you make the dipping sauce (below) and cut up the greens and meat.

Dipping sauce

Mix 5 tablespoons water, 3 tablespoons sugar, 2 tablespoons vinegar and 2 tablespoons fish sauce. Add to this a little finely chopped garlic and chilli.

Cooking

Add some oil to a non-stick pan on medium heat, then fry a sprinkling of onions, meat and bean sprouts. Pour a thin layer of batter on top of all this. Leave it to cook well (cover if needed). Once the edges look done, flip one half over the other (like a circle folded in half).

Serve

Stack the cooked pancakes and serve with the sauce and any greens you like for crunch.

4. Felt Pen Pigments Experiment (DIY Chromatography)

What you need

- coffee filter paper
- mixture of felt pens
- cup
- water

What to do

Along the bottom edge of the coffee filter paper (but not on the crinkly bits) put a row of different coloured dots about half a centimetre wide. Leave a centimetre between them. Put a small amount of water into a wide cup or plastic container. Sit the filter paper upright so that just the bottom edge touches the water. The dots should be above, not under the waterline. Wait and watch the patterns unfurl.

What's happening?

As the water is drawn up through the paper, it dissolves the inks and they join it for the journey. But the individual pigments that were mixed together to make each colour move at different speeds through the paper. None of them can move as fast as the water, so they separate and spread out like a colourful smear. Scientists use chromatography (but not with coffee filters) to separate and analyse all kinds of mixtures, not just felt pen colours.

See you next time!